DARK SHORE

A LANCE BRODY NOVEL (BOOK 3)

MICHAEL ROBERTSON, JR.

ISBN: 9781717863522

DARK SHORE

THEM
(I)

PETE SIMPSON WAS FLIPPING THROUGH A *PLAYBOY* magazine—yes, an actual magazine, circa 1996, with faded, heavily creased pages, but fortunately none stuck together by suspicious means—and casting repeated glances at the clock on the wall, waiting impatiently for seven o'clock.

Simpson's Garage and Used Auto closed at seven on the weekdays and four on Saturday, and it was closed on Sunday, praise Jesus. Pete wasn't the Simpson the ancient sign out front referred to. That would be his father, Marvin Simpson—Marv, to most everyone in town. But ole Marv, who'd be seventy-one next spring, liked to check out around three most days now, leaving the garage, and the auto sales, in the charge of his only son, Pete. Not because he really trusted him, Pete suspected, but because Marv was just too damned old and tired to care that much anymore.

Pete, who would turn thirty-seven the day after Marvin turned seventy-one, leaned back in the squeaky, stained office chair in the long-outdated front office space of Simpson's Garage and Used Auto, with a half-hard penis—thanks in part to the centerfold of Miss June, 1996—and zero ambition to do anything else in his life except lock the door come closing time, climb into his pickup truck and drive home to his one-bedroom on Spruce Street—a whole four blocks from his childhood home —and down a couple cold ones while he watched ESPN before falling asleep on the couch, only to wake up in the morning and drive back to the garage for another day of oil changes, spark plugs, tire rotations, and disappointed glances from his father.

At ten till seven, Pete had just decided to reach his hand down his pants and finish the job that Miss June had started.

That was when the door to the office opened slowly, the tarnished bell mounted above the door frame giving off a ring that startled Pete so badly he jumped from the chair, pulling his grease-stained hand free from the waistband of his workpants and flinging the magazine to the floor in front of him, hidden from view behind a chipped wooden desk.

"We're closed!" was all he could manage to say, flustered and with cheeks burning. "We're closed, dammit!"

The man who'd come through the door turned and gently closed it. He was fairly tall and dressed just like Father Abrams down at Holy Name of Mary. An establishment Pete hadn't stepped foot in since his old sleepover days with Jimmy May, when Jimmy's parents would wake the two of them up after a night of playing Nintendo and drag them down the street to say, "Peace be with you," and do funny things with their hands across their chests.

"The sign on the door says you close at seven o'clock," the Reverend said. "Trust me, that's more time than I need."

As the Reverend walked across the office toward him, Pete Simpson used the toe of his work boot to slowly slide the magazine under the desk in a manner he hoped was inconspicuous. Apparently, he failed, because as the man approached, he said, "Partaking in a little sin of the flesh this evening, Peter?"

Pete crinkled his brow and cocked his head to the side. Nobody had called him Peter since his grandmother had passed. And how in the hell did this man know his name? He wasn't from here, no way. Town this small, Pete would have seen him before. Maybe he was new? Maybe Father Abrams had finally decided to move on from his flock, move to Miami or somewhere else in Florida to sit on beaches and contemplate committing his own sins of the flesh?

It was possible, sure. But if there was one thing that was true about Simpson's Garage and Used Auto, it was that, much like at the local barbershop, it was a place men would gather around cups of coffee while their cars were getting worked on, or while they decided to hang out for a spell when they came to pick up the parts they'd special-ordered, and they'd gossip just as readily as any group of women you could come across. Pete suspected this constant chatter and slipstream of local information and misinformation was the only thing that kept his pop coming in every day. If Father Abrams was leaving the church, Pete would have heard about it.

The Reverend said, "Don't worry, Peter. I'm not here to judge you."

And when the man did not stop in front of the desk, but instead came around the side and stepped toward him, Pete felt a sudden compulsion to take a step back. No, it was more than a compulsion. When the man had taken that last step in his direction, Pete had felt as if some invisible force, like a strong gust of wind, had physically moved his body backward. He stumbled and landed in the old office chair, which caught him gracefully and wheeled backward a foot before coming to rest against the wall.

The Reverend stooped with a deftness that seemed to defy his age and appearance and plucked the *Playboy* from the floor, using the back of one hand to brush off the dust and dirt that had adhered to the cover. He held it out in front of him for a moment, eyes flitting over the image and the taglines for articles nobody would ever read, and then flipped through the pages until he found the centerfold. He gave the picture of Miss June a long stare, allowing himself this momentary pleasure, and then turned the magazine around and held it up so Pete could see.

Pete's eyes instantly locked onto the woman in the magazine.

"Do you like her, Peter?" the Reverend asked, taking a small step closer.

Pete nodded his head. Found himself sinking deeper into the magazine picture, unable to avert his gaze.

"What is it you like about her, Peter?"

Pete felt his vision narrow, as if the office was closing in around him. Things began to fade away, a blackness creeping in from the sides. His body felt slack, a calm washing over him the way it used to when he'd gotten slightly addicted to Xanax, before his pop had figured out what was going on and threatened his life. He tried to answer, tried to form words and found he could only utter a low grunt.

The Reverend took another step closer and held the magazine out. "I think she likes you, too, Peter."

The blackness was creeping in closer now. The only color left in the world was the picture of the naked woman in front of him. And boy, did he want her. Wanted her bad. His mind filled with wild fantasies of the two of them, and he felt his penis grow again in his pants.

"You can have her, Peter." The man's voice invaded his thoughts, carved its way through his mind. "She's all yours."

On the page, Pete would swear the woman's face came alive. That she winked at him, and then bit her lower lip in a way that suggested she wanted him just as badly as he was lusting after her.

"But first," the Reverend said, looming over his prey, "tell me where you keep the keys to the cars you're selling."

———

The Reverend stepped outside, gently closing the door to Simpson's Garage and Used Auto behind him and tossing a small key ring with two silver keys attached to it to the Surfer, who was sitting on the hood of a beaten-down Ford Taurus for sale, with his flip-flop-clad feet up on the bumper and his palms flat on the hood at his sides.

In the cone of yellow light falling across him from the overhead parking lot lamp, the Surfer looked like a model for some vintage beach advertisement. Board shorts to go along with the flip-flops, cutoff t-shirt exposing well-muscled and deeply tanned skin, and shoulder-length blond hair to round out the appearance. He looked ready for the sand and the waves. No matter that winter was fast approaching and the temperature was currently somewhere in the midforties. The Reverend didn't understand everything about the Surfer—not even close, he sometimes hated to admit to himself. But of all the burning questions, the fact that the Surfer never seemed to be affected by the weather was perhaps one of the most puzzling.

The Surfer snatched the keys from the air and jumped off the hood. "You get it?"

"Read the tag," the Reverend said, nodding to the key ring.

The Surfer held the key ring up and examined a small plastic tag attached along with the keys. He nodded. "Righteous."

It was something they should have done sooner, dumping the Volkswagen bus. The Reverend knew this, but he'd taken a calculated risk. They'd gotten so close to obtaining the boy that he hadn't wanted to waste time trying to figure out other suitable transportation. He'd wanted to stay after the boy while the trail might still be fresh.

So close, he thought, a quick pang of anger suddenly surfacing.

They'd finally tracked the boy down to Hillston, Virginia, and the first time the Reverend had laid eyes on him, he had seen the power and the energy and the ... *aura* that the boy put out, and he couldn't help but smile. *He's the one*, the Reverend had thought that day. *He's the one who will finally make it possible.*

But then, on the night they'd attempted to obtain the boy, everything had gone wrong in one single act of unexpected, unforeseen defiance by the boy's mother that was so profound the Reverend still had a hard time bringing himself to believe it had happened the way it had.

Love was a dreadfully powerful emotion. One he'd never understand.

Because of what had happened that night in Hillston, each day they continued driving the orange-and-white Volkswagen bus was a day they were inviting trouble. Surely the vehicle was on the state police's list of vehicles to be on the lookout for, and it wasn't exactly nondescript. But the Surfer had loved that vehicle, and while the Reverend wasn't the sentimental type, he did feel that good work deserved rewarding. And the Surfer had definitely done good work over the years. Strange, mystifying work, but good all the same.

But it had to be done. It was a risk to the overall goal, and after very little coaxing, the Surfer had been in agreement.

They'd removed the license plates and tossed them into two separate dumpsters at two different fast-food restaurants along the interstate. Then, an hour ago, after the sun had completely set, they'd driven it to a campsite near the river they'd seen advertised on billboards as they'd driven north, parked it, and simply walked away.

It had taken half an hour to walk along a winding mountain road to get back to the outskirts of this little town, and as their good luck would have it, only another five minutes before they'd come across Simpson's Garage and Used Auto.

They'd both stopped along the sidewalk, turned to look out at all the clunkers and tossed-away cars in the crushed gravel lot. The Surfer had pointed and said, "That one."

The Reverend had looked to where he was pointing and rolled his eyes. Then he'd spied Peter Simpson through the blinds of the office building. He studied the man for a moment, reaching out to get a sense of him, and then said, "Let's see if I can strike us a good deal."

Which he had. And Pete Simpson wouldn't remember a thing, except a very vivid dream involving Miss June, 1996, and a sudden urge to go to the Holy Name of Mary Catholic Church and confess his sins to Father Abrams.

———

A moment later, a Honda Element in better-than-expected condition pulled out of the Simpson's Garage and Used Auto sales lot and drove north through town, turning onto the rural route that would eventually lead to the interstate onramp. Its driver and passenger both sat quietly, eyes focused straight ahead, their mission resumed.

In the moonlight, the car's bluish-green color appeared almost metallic.

It might remind you of the ocean.

[1]

As the bus slowed to make the turn, allowing Lance Brody to catch a long glimpse of the wooden sign posted at the city limits welcoming visitors to Sugar Beach, all he could think was, *I am in desperate need of coffee.* This thought was followed by a funny image of a shoreline where the sand was replaced by actual sugar, full of kids shoving fistfuls of the stuff into their mouths while they built towering sugar castles, and teenagers riding chocolate sauce waves on surfboard-shaped lollipops. The seagulls flying overhead raining down dollops of frosting instead of ... well, you know.

Lance was quickly pulled away from this happy if not ridiculous image by an all-too-familiar feeling in the pit of his stomach. An ever-so-faint tingling at the base of his skull. Just like migraine sufferers who could often feel the early warning signs of an oncoming attack, Lance Brody was developing a much stronger sense of awareness as well.

He was starting to more easily detect when and where he was needed.

He often didn't fully understand it, nor necessarily agree with it. But he could not deny it, nor could he ignore it.

Not after the sacrifice his mother had made for him. Not after she'd ended her life in the effort to make sure Lance got out into the world to use his gifts and his talents and his abilities for good. Too help stave off the Evil that lurked beyond the veil and snaked its way out into our realm.

And sadly, there was plenty of Evil to go around. Of both the otherworldly *and* the human variety. Lance often wondered whether, if human beings knew how many threats and how much darkness surrounded them, hunted them, fed on them, if they would still be so terrible to each other. Cause so much pain amongst themselves and hurt each other so badly, in such grotesque ways.

He was confident the answer was yes. Yes, they would. Which was a thought that made him so sad he had to quickly push it away whenever it decided to surface.

Lance was good at pushing thoughts away. You could almost go ahead and label it as one of his gifts. It was part of his survival instinct, part of what allowed him to go on each and every day, carrying the burden of abilities he'd been born with.

Growing up, once he'd reached a certain age, he had begun pushing away thoughts of any type of future outside his hometown. He'd turned down the basketball scholarships, to the tune of many grumbling voices from coaches on the other end of the phone. At the time, he'd deemed moving on too risky. His abilities kept him busy enough at home, and there, he was comfortable—at least as comfortable as he could be—with managing them. The thought of going out into the great big unknown world had seemed overwhelming. Plus, he didn't think he could ever bring himself to leave his mother. Not after all she'd done for him. Though Lance knew what he was born with was not necessarily his fault, he still often felt the twinge of guilt. Guilt that, because of what he was, he'd kept his mother from living a fuller life, going out and seeing the world, or dating again.

But now she was gone, and though the feelings of guilt and sadness still took up residence in the back of Lance's mind, buried beneath everything he could find to pile on top of them, his mother had become one of the thoughts he had to push away so frequently it sometimes felt like a betrayal.

When he did think of her, he tried to focus on the bright spots—the happy memories, of which there'd been plenty. But the final memory of them together was the one that usually butted its ugly face into his mind. The image of her broken and bleeding body lying in the parking lot adjacent to the Great Hillston Cemetery, dying in his arms. The words she'd offered with her dying breath—*Go, Lance. It's only what's right. I love you.*

She'd sacrificed herself for him. Died so he could live, though Lance didn't find it quite as biblical as that. But though his mother had made her choice—urged on by influences Lance did not fully understand, no matter how many times he'd replayed the scene of Pamela Brody gripping the wrought-iron fence of the Great Hillston Cemetery, head bowed as if in prayer, while what looked like hundreds of spirits stood stoic beyond the fence and all whispered in unison—in Lance's mind, she had been murdered.

The Reverend and the Surfer had killed her.

And while Lance had no substantial evidence, he knew without question that they were still after him. Hunting him down.

Which was why he'd fled his hometown and had bounced from bus to bus, town to town, ever since. Stopping where he felt he needed to, and then moving on again.

It was why he'd left Leah behind in Westhaven. Until he had a better understanding of what he was really up against, he could not endanger her like that, and also could not create such a liability for himself. It was easier this way, if not also incredibly more difficult.

But there was a shimmer of light in that tunnel. After another near-death experience in the small town of Ripton's Grove, two new friends had inspired Lance to come to a new conclusion about his relationship with Leah. Whereas his initial instinct was to seal the memory of her off completely, a sort of all-or-nothing approach, Lance had had the realization that maybe, just maybe, it was okay to allow himself a small pleasure. He could not survive the rest of his life never allowing himself to have friends. If that was the case, he might as well allow the Reverend and the Surfer to come get him and do whatever it was they wanted. Life without any joy, even if only the smallest amount, is a life not worth living.

So, as he'd taken a seat on another bus, headed toward another town, he'd pulled his out-of-date flip phone from his pocket and sent Leah a message.

Her response had come so quickly, Lance couldn't help but laugh.

I miss you, too!!!

Three exclamation marks. That had to count for something.

The bus hopped over two speed bumps as it pulled into the parking lot of a bus station so brightly lit with fluorescents and neon signage that Lance felt he needed sunglasses, despite the nearly hidden sun as dusk dissolved to night. The airbrakes hissed and the bus driver welcomed them all to Sugar Beach with about as much enthusiasm as someone might inform you they were headed off to get a root canal, and then the big bus door swung open and people began to amble off.

Lance Brody waited his turn, then grabbed his backpack from the seat next to him, thanked the driver, and made his way down the steps. The feeling at the base of his skull was still there, but for now, Lance was ignoring it. It'd been a long trip, and now, before anything else, he needed coffee.

Sugar Beach was a small touristy town on the coast of Maryland, not quite an hour north of Ocean City, tucked away on the edge of the peninsula. Lance only knew this because, after he'd purchased his ticket at the last depot, he'd had close to a two-hour wait before his bus departed. He'd spent some time walking around the mostly empty bus station and had stumbled upon a wire display rack that housed magazines for sale, as well as travel atlases that were grimy with dust. After studying the map of Maryland for a moment, he'd replaced the atlas on the rack, and for the first time since the night his mother had died, he'd had a clear understanding of exactly where he was headed. Directionally, at least.

He hadn't left the state of Virginia since high school, and he was oddly at peace with the idea of moving on, if not a bit somber.

"Headed to Sugar Beach, son?"

A man, maybe seventy years old, in a heavy sweater and corduroy pants with loafers on his feet, was sitting on a bench nearby, a paperback novel facedown on his lap. Before Lance could answer, the man offered, "Make sure you get crabs."

"Sorry?" Lance said.

"Sugar Beach has the best crabs you can eat. Softshell, crab legs, crab cakes, you name it. Beats the pants off the bigger commercial places south of 'em."

And with that, the man went back to his novel.

Lance chose a bench three down for the remainder of his wait, thinking that *Make sure you get crabs* would maybe make the world's worst t-shirt.

Like a lot of things, Lance couldn't explain the decision to buy the ticket to Sugar Beach. All he could say for sure was that, after the bus had pulled into the station and he'd stepped down onto the sidewalk, his first inclination had been to head right inside and move on, and then suddenly he had been standing in front of a ticket window, scanning names of cities on the departures list, and had heard the words *Sugar Beach* pass his lips.

Despite the loneliness that often weighed Lance down, he could never say he was truly alone. The Universe was always there, pushing, pulling, suggesting. It had saved him. It had infuriated him. It had baffled him. Lance would even go so far to say it had *joked* with him.

But one thing Lance would not concede was that the Universe had ever actually guided him. Because that would be too easy, right? Lance still had to keep up his end of the unspoken bargain. He was the soldier, and the Universe was more the general.

And now here he was, in a new town—a new *state*—with the all-too-familiar feeling growing inside him. The general, letting him know it was time to assemble the troops. Though maybe it was nothing. Maybe Lance was only meant to arrive in Sugar Beach for some R&R, get some rest before heading off to the next thing, whatever that might be. It wouldn't be the first stop he'd taken that would begin and end without dilemma or disaster or an agenda.

As Lance watched the elderly man in the sweater and corduroys amble off down the sidewalk and round the corner out of sight, he thought, *Maybe I'm just here for the crabs. That would be a nice change.*

The bus station, like many, as Lance had come to learn, was on the outskirts of the town. An old building with a fading façade and weathered features. Neon signs glowed in the windows, advertising parasailing, charter fishing, golf, and the

ever-tacky t-shirts and souvenirs, desperate to catch newly
arrived tourists with newly arrived dollars. There was a timeshare sales office attached to the far end of the building, but its
window blinds were drawn shut, its door chained, and a sign
posted in the window reading *Closed for the season. See you in
the spring!*

Lance looked at the chain on the door for a long time. When
he turned back around to survey the parking lot, he realized his
bus was the only one on the large expanse of asphalt, engine
purring as it idled like a lone beast resting in its den. He counted
six cars in the parking lot and had to wonder how many
belonged to bus station employees.

Off-season, Lance thought. *Maybe this will be a quiet stop
after all.*

He turned and pushed inside the bus station's double doors
and was greeted with the smell of cleaning solution and salt-
water taffy. The space was large and open, with bright overhead
lights and a white floor that looked freshly mopped. The walls
were adorned with posters showing families and couples smiling
and laughing as they played in pools and on beaches, dined
together at seafood restaurants and stared up at the darkened
sky in awe as fireworks decorated the night.

They all looked so happy, so in love with each other. So free.

Lance looked past them, blocked out the projected happiness, and found the sign pointing to the restrooms, which were
located down a small alcove next to a gift shop that suggested
Lance should BOOK AN EXCURSION NOW! in the form of
a flashing digital sign in the window. Lance headed toward it,
passing by the ticket window with a middle-aged woman behind
the glass, her feet on the desk and an iPad in her lap. She was
flicking brightly colored fruit around the screen. She sat up as
Lance passed. He nodded and smiled, and when she realized he
wasn't stopping, she continued with her game.

The door to the gift shop was locked—no chain here, just a simple deadbolt—and the interior was all darkness and the vague outlines of shelving and clothes racks. Likely full of the t-shirts and souvenirs promised by the outside window.

Lance made his way down the alcove and found the men's room. There was a small janitorial closet located at the end of the hall with a mop bucket propping it open, shelves full of cleaning agents and supplies weakly illuminated by an overhead lamp.

He pushed through the men's room door and found a man dressed in faded blue work pants and matching shirt washing his hands rigorously at the sink, soap thickly lathered and water steaming hot. Their eyes met in the mirror. The man's face was sun-damaged and heavily wrinkled, but Lance guessed he wasn't more than forty years old. His eyes were bloodshot, but looked very much alive. Lance nodded a hello, and then moved to slide past the man in search of a urinal.

The man stood from the sink and turned, the water still running full blast, steam still billowing from the basin, and blocked Lance's way. Not aggressively, not exactly, but Lance took a step back all the same. The man's bloodshot eyes took Lance in, head to foot, as if performing some sort of inspection.

Then, as casually as he might ask Lance if he'd like a stick of gum, the man asked, "Did you come here to die?"

[2]

LANCE WAS TIRED.

He'd been riding busses for nearly twenty-four hours and had slept little. He hated to sound giddy, but something about Leah's text message response to him—(*I miss you, too!!!*)—had stirred up some sort of adrenaline in him. It was different from the types of instant energy he'd been used to. The ones that had given him his second wind on the basketball court as a close game came down to the wire, or, most recently, the kind that pushed his legs a little harder, gave his muscles a little more strength as he fought or fled for his life. This new type of feeling that rushed through him was more euphoric. It was driven by happiness, followed by his mind wandering off into daydreams of a life he wanted, with the girl he wanted. He'd allowed himself these moments, isolated on a bus ambling down a highway with nothing but his thoughts to occupy him. But eventually, the rush faded, the bus slowed, and now here he was, tired and in need of caffeine or a bed, whichever came first.

Which was why Lance was certain he had misheard the man in the bus station men's room.

"Sorry?" Lance asked, taking another small step backward.

The man in the blue work outfit, presumably the handler of the mop bucket out in the hallway, didn't hesitate. Repeated himself again with the same nonchalance.

"Did you come here to die?" The way he said it, he might have been asking if Lance wanted fries to go along with his burger.

Though Lance's battery was drained, he didn't sense any real threat from the man in front of him. He didn't appear aggressive, he didn't even seem to be that interested in Lance's answer. He stood patiently, still blocking Lance's path to the row of urinals along the far wall. Lance strained his mind, trying to come up with some sort of scenario where any of this made sense, and finally gave up.

"Umm, no, thank you. I actually came here to pee."

The man waited a beat, let his eyes do another slide up and down Lance's body, then nodded.

"My mistake," he said and finished washing his hands. He dried them with a handful of paper towels and then, without another word, slid past Lance and left the restroom.

Lance stood in place for another moment, trying to figure out if the conversation had really happened. Then he looked at himself in one of the mirrors above the sink, shrugged, and finally made his way to the urinal.

When he left the restroom, he found that the mop bucket was gone and the door to the storage room was closed, a placard reading STAFF ONLY thwarting curious hands. Lance made his way down the short alcove, passed the locked-up gift shop where he could book his excursions, and then stopped at the ticket window. The woman with the iPad flicked some more digital fruit across the screen before placing the device on the counter and standing to greet him.

"How can I help you?" she asked, her eyes narrowing slightly as she took in the sight of him, as if it was difficult to focus on the real world after staring at a screen for so long. On the other side of the glass partition, Lance felt a bit like a zoo exhibit as the woman studied him.

Lance adjusted the straps of his backpack and leaned down a little to speak through the tiny metal grate. "Yes, ma'am. I was hoping you could direct me to a place to get a decent cup of coffee." Then he added, "And possibly suggest a place to stay the night. Nothing fancy, but hopefully clean."

The woman's hair was pulled back in a loose ponytail, gray roots peeking out. She wore very little makeup, with no jewelry, and while her face betrayed her boredom at sitting behind the little counter in an empty bus station all evening, when she let a small grin escape, Lance could see was actually very pretty. But still, there was something sad in her eyes.

"There's a diner a mile from here, right on the corner of Sand Dollar Road and Highway 19. It doesn't look like much—nothing around here really does—but their coffee will kick you in the face. You know, in a good way."

Lance nodded and smiled. "Sounds perfect."

"As far as where you can stay ... how long are you planning to be here?"

Something in her voice was funny to Lance, suggesting maybe there was a lot more to the question than Lance could see on the surface.

He answered the way he often answered questions. "I don't know."

She eyed him again, and Lance put on a smile and shrugged. Something about his answer, or his unwillingness to elaborate more on her question, must have set something off, because instead of making a suggestion, she pulled a brochure from one of the drawers beneath her counter and slid it through the small opening at the bottom of the window.

"Just stay away from any of the places on Riptide Lane, they're dumps. Most all the other motels are about the same."

Lance nodded again. "No Riptide Lane. Got it. Thank you, ma'am. Have a good evening. Good luck with your fruit."

He turned to leave and was halfway across the newly mopped white floor when he heard a door open behind him and the woman called out, "Hey!"

Lance stopped and turned, found the woman sticking her head out an opened door a few feet down from the ticket window. He met her eyes and again saw something that looked like sadness.

"What's your name?" she asked.

Lance hesitated for just a second, then said, "Lance, ma'am."

The woman pushed the rest of the way through the door and hurried after him. When she reached him, she wrapped her arms around him in a hug, giving him one gentle squeeze before pulling away and saying, "My name's Barb, and I just want you to know that somebody out there loves you, Lance."

Then she patted his arm, smiled, and made her way back through the office door and out of sight.

Lance's first thought after the woman's proclamation was of Leah, and how if there was somebody out there thinking about him right now, he wanted it to be her. He didn't know if Leah loved him—they'd only known each other a few days, after all—but he was confident she cared about him, at the least.

Lance's second thought was that the two people he'd met so far in Sugar Beach sure did have some strange ideas about what casual conversation needed to be.

[3]

THE SUN WAS COMPLETELY GONE WHEN LANCE PUSHED through the bus station door and found himself back in the parking lot. The bus he'd ridden in on was gone, either pulled around back somewhere for the evening or off to another city, another town, part of someone else's story. The sky was cloudless and the stars popped like diamonds on black velvet. Lance could smell the ocean in the air, salt and sand, and he wondered just how close he was to the shoreline and the high tide.

He pulled his flip phone from his pocket and saw it was almost six thirty. A steady stream of cars was passing by on the road, headed into town. Commuters on their way home, maybe. If Barb hadn't informed Lance that his cup of coffee was a mile away, he seriously would have considered hitchhiking. It was something he'd never done before, but right now he was running dangerously low on fuel. His body seemed heavy, and his thoughts were getting loose.

A breeze blew across the parking lot, throwing the strong scent of the ocean into Lance's face. He inhaled deeply, filling his lungs, and then set off toward the road. A sidewalk carried him toward town, headlights growing and shrinking Lance's silhouette on the ground as they passed him one by one. Some-body honked, and Lance heard a group of girls' laughter from an opened window as the vehicle sped by, a pop song turned up on the radio.

Lance passed a battered road sign telling him he was walking parallel to Highway 19, and after another couple minutes saw the bright neon sign of the diner on the corner of an intersection with a traffic light swaying slightly in the breeze.

Lance stood at the corner and looked down Sand Dollar Road. Lit up bright as it was, the diner stood on the corner like the welcome sign to Sugar Beach. The starting gate to the rest the town had to offer. Beyond it was a long stretch of other businesses: restaurants, motels, surf shops, and a large empty parking lot with a sign so large and so well lit, Lance could read it all the way from the corner—**BEACH ACCESS - $10 ALL DAY PARKING.**

There was music playing from somewhere down the street, loud and with a strong country twang. A sports bar, maybe. If Sugar Beach had a main strip, Lance was pretty sure he'd just found it.

The diner was perfectly named Sugar Beach Diner and advertised this in bright pink neon atop the roofline. The exterior was all big windows and dull aluminum, which reflected the pink from the sign and the glow from inside in a slightly disorienting sparkling effect. The parking lot was fuller than Lance had been expecting, given how empty the bus station had been, and as he stepped over the curb, he saw the car that'd honked at him parked crookedly along the front of the building. Through one of the big windows, Lance saw a group of four young women, no more than twenty, surely, huddled together in a booth on the right, laughing and flipping through the oversized menus.

He made a note to ask for a table on the left of the restaurant. He wasn't in the mood to try and drown out highly energized high-pitched voices.

He just wanted coffee. The biggest they could legally give him.

Lance was almost to the door when something stopped him. A noise, somewhere to his left. Somebody had coughed. The sound was from deep down, one of those rattling coughs that brought to mind images of little pebbles shaking around in a burlap bag.

A shape took form in the darkness, lit only by the glow that reached it from the diner, and the ever-changing red, green and yellow of the stoplight above. On the opposite corner, across the street from the diner, somebody was huddled inside a sweatshirt, the hood pulled up and cinched around their face. They sat on the corner of the sidewalk atop what looked like a rolling suitcase, holding what could only be a sheet of cardboard or poster board with some words scrawled on it.

Another cough started and was drowned out in the sound of an approaching stream of cars as the light changed. Lance watched as the hooded figure stood from where they'd sat and held the sign up as cars began to stop at the opposite light that had just turned red.

Lance stood, rooted in place, watching as the figure walked tentatively toward the first car in line and held the sign out, then slowly walked past it and toward the rest of the waiting cars.

The light changed, and the cars moved on. Nobody had offered anything to the hooded figure, who walked back to the suitcase and sat once again, setting the cardboard sign at their feet and pulling their hands inside the sleeves of the sweatshirt.

Lance wore cargo shorts and his hoodie, and while the breeze had a little bite to it, he wasn't cold. Rarely was, actually. But as he watched the figure on the corner attempt to pull themselves further inside their sweatshirt, he had to wonder just how long they'd been sitting there.

The diner's door opened, and a man came out, talking loudly on a cell phone. Something about making sure the buyer had the money in escrow no later than Thursday. Lance caught a whiff of food from the open door and went inside, casting another glance over his shoulder toward the figure on the corner as he did.

Since the diner was moderately busy, and the staff was likely used to catering to a never-ending revolution of tourists, nobody really seemed to pay much attention to Lance, for which he was thankful. Since the night his mother had died, he felt as though he carried around a weight of paranoia and an ever-present need to look over his shoulder, check his blind spots, consider strangers suspect. Something about the steady hum of energy in the diner coupled with the aroma of food and, thank goodness, coffee allowed him a moment of reprieve. His concerns melted a bit, and when the waitress brought him the coffee he'd ordered, he took the first sip, bathed in the rush of pleasure it brought him, and leaned his head against the upholstered seatback and actually sighed.

He took another sip, swallowed, and smiled. Barb had been correct. The coffee kicked you in the teeth. In the best of ways.

He ordered chicken pot pie with a side salad and devoured the food as though it were a contest. His coffee was refilled twice, and when the waitress asked if he'd like dessert, he asked if they had pie.

They did. Five different kinds. Lance chose a slice of apple and a slice of chocolate mousse.

"One to go?" the waitress had asked.

"No, ma'am. Both for here, please," Lance answered. And with the question came a thought. Lance looked out the window to his right, turned half around in his seat to look toward the stoplight. Through the glare on the window, he could just make out the hooded figure, still seated on the rolling suitcase. "But I'll take two to-go cups of coffee, if you have them, please."

The waitress nodded and headed off, returning with his order in record time.

Lance enjoyed the pie, though the chocolate mousse was a little too artificial-tasting for his liking, downed the rest of his coffee, and then scooped up his check and the two Styrofoam to-go cups and walked to the checkout counter near the entrance.

There was a short line of people waiting to pay, and Lance stood patiently, double-fisting coffee cups like he was about to pull an all-nighter cramming for exams. As he inched his way forward, one successful transaction at a time, he eyed a bulletin board on the wall behind the cash register. Various flyers were hung skewed and haphazardly, multicolored pushpins peppering the board and keeping them in place. There were flyers for timeshare rentals, boat rentals, charter fishing trips, beach yoga, and a coed volleyball team. Most of the flyers looked tired and out-of-date. Probably put up during the busy spring and summer months and now forgotten.

One in particular drew Lance's attention. It was a solid white sheet of paper with a red heart that looked like it had been painted in watercolor. The advertising text below the image left no room for interpretation. It simply gave the phone number for a suicide prevention hotline.

It seemed incredibly out of place among all the other flyers advertising fun and adventurous activities. But, Lance thought, maybe that was the point. A statement being made.

He paid cash, left a nice tip for the waitress, and then used his shoulder to push through the door and back into the cool evening air.

The temperature seemed to have dropped almost ten degrees from earlier, and ordinarily Lance might have decided to pull his hood up to help keep his ears warm. But right now, two things kept that from happening. First, both his hands were full as he carried the two Styrofoam cups of coffee across the parking lot. Second, when he approached the figure huddled beneath the stoplight, he didn't want to appear to be a threat. He wanted his face visible and his hands out in the open, coffee or not.

There was no crosswalk here, but there was also no traffic. The steady stream of cars that had crisscrossed the road earlier was all but gone. As Lance jogged across the black seam of road, he saw a single pair of headlights glowing in the distance, growing from the blackness that was the opposite end of Sand Dollar Road, away from all the motels and business and country music. There was nothing there that Lance could see. Nothing except the two glowing eyes of the car getting closer and closer as he walked the last twenty-five feet or so up the sidewalk and stopped beside the hooded figure.

The first thing Lance noticed was that the person wasn't sitting on a rolling suitcase. It was actually a rolling cooler, something you might load up with a bag of ice and a few sodas for a family road trip, or a day at the ballfield ... or a day at the beach.

The second thing Lance noticed was the wisps of long blond hair escaping the hoodie the figure had pulled up on their head, the red stoplight above highlighting them a deep shade of crimson.

At the sound of Lance's approaching footsteps, the figure turned atop the cooler, took in his presence and stood quickly, taking a fast step backward and dropping the cardboard sign at her feet.

The quickness of her movement had caused the hood of the sweatshirt to fall slightly, exposing one half of her head and face. She reached up and jerked the other half down, shook her hair free and eyed Lance like somebody who was used to a fight. Ready to react.

Her eyes were so blue they pierced the night. Burned straight through the red glow of the stoplight.

She might have been eighteen, or maybe twenty-five. It was impossible to tell. She looked youthful, but also aged, as if life had been unkind. Stolen some precious years. Her blond hair fell past her shoulders, naturally curling at the bottom.

She was beautiful. Strikingly so.

But there was something else.

Lance stood still, tried his best to smile despite the strong sense of sadness he felt pulsing off this girl. It struck him deep in the gut like a dull knife, and he had to work hard to clear his throat and say, "I brought you a coffee."

No response from the girl.

Lance shrugged. "I just figured it was cold out here and you might like something warm. I, uh, well, I can just leave it here on your cooler, if you'd like."

He took one half-step forward, never breaking eye contact as he bent at the knees and gently set one of the to-go cups atop the hard plastic lid of the cooler. When he stood, the headlights of the car that had been approaching from the dead side of Sand Dollar Road splashed across his face and then homed in on the girl in front of him as the vehicle braked and came to a slow stop.

The girl turned and saw the car, a solid black Ford Excursion that looked like somebody could live inside it and probably took a gallon of gas just to start up and back down the driveway.

The girl looked back to Lance, her gaze accompanied by a stab of fear—only not of him. It was almost as if the fear was *for* him.

"Thank you," she said, with some sort of accent, heavy and thick, that took Lance by surprise. Something European, maybe? Her words were short and clipped and meant to dismiss, as if she were trying to move Lance along.

Something else about the situation had changed, and it took Lance a moment to recognize what was wrong. The red glow of the stoplight was no more, having shifted to a bright green that cast a limelike hue across the scene.

The light was green.

Lance didn't drive often, but he'd retained enough knowledge from driver's education to know that a green light meant go. The black Ford Excursion was not going. It continued to sit, dark-tinted windows making it impossible to tell if the driver was looking down at their phone, had suffered a heart attack, or was sitting and staring out the window, watching, waiting.

Everything suddenly felt very bad, and Lance decided he had seen enough. Or rather, it was as though Lance was being told he'd seen enough.

"You're welcome," he said to the girl.

He gave the driver's-side window of the Ford one more glance, hoping to catch a glimpse of something, *anything*, and saw nothing but darkness.

Lance Brody jogged back across the street toward the diner's parking lot, leaving the beautiful girl in the green glow of the traffic light and the heavy shadow of the SUV.

[4]

THERE WAS A SMALL SIDEWALK THAT LINED THE FRONT OF the diner, and Lance stopped on the corner of it, kneeling down and pretending to search for something inside his backpack while keeping his eyes in the direction of the girl beneath the stoplight. The light had turned red again, and three cars drove past on the Highway 19, temporarily obscuring Lance's view. When they'd passed, the girl had made her way back to the rolling cooler. She removed the to-go cup of coffee and set it on the sidewalk, then grabbed one of the cooler's handles with one hand and scooped the cardboard sign from the sidewalk with the other.

As she started toward the Excursion, cooler in tow, the back hatch of the vehicle opened automatically, slowing rising up like a mouth about to swallow her. She bent and lifted the cooler from the ground, struggling against the weight of whatever was inside, balance wobbling briefly as she straightened and just managed to rest the cooler on the lip of the rear opening, sliding it inside and tossing the sign in after it. Then she reached up and pressed a button on the hatch and it began to close again, just as lazily as it had opened.

She walked around to the passenger side of the vehicle, out of sight. When the light turned green, the black Excursion drove through the intersection at a speed which felt very slow to Lance. *Yep. They're definitely checking me out.*

Not one to shy away from a moment, Lance smiled and waved a farewell to the SUV as if it were driven by a longtime friend.

He had to assume the driver did not wave back. He didn't even get a friendly toot of the horn.

Lance's eyes followed the Excursion down Sand Dollar Road until it eventually turned off onto another street, the image of the girl's face, those piercing eyes, refusing to leave his mind.

"She's hot, right?"

Lance spun around at the sound of the voice, not realizing anybody had been nearby. Down the side of the diner, a utility door, presumably leading into the kitchen, was propped open with a plastic milk crate. Easy access to the dumpster and grease disposal bin that sat huddled in the corner of the rear lot. A young man leaned against the wall, one leg bent, foot against the aluminum siding. His head was resting back, looking up to the sky as he exhaled a puff of smoke while flicking the ash from the cigarette he pinched in his left hand. He wore jeans with black rubber nonslip shoes and a white t-shirt, with a black apron draped around his neck and cinched around the waist.

"What's that?" Lance said, taking a step closer.

The man took another drag from his cigarette and then extinguished it on a small plastic ashtray atop the upturned milk crate. Exhaled the smoke and said, "The girl on the corner. She's a hottie, right? Those eyes are something else."

The man turned to look at Lance, and in the moonlight, Lance figured the guy was midtwenties at the most. Close to Lance's own age.

"Who is she?" Lance asked, walking closer and leaning his shoulder against the side of the building, trying to look relaxed, trying to keep his words full of just the right amount of curiosity. Just a young guy asking about an attractive girl. Not a telepathic soldier of the Universe's army who talked to the dead in his free time. Because there was no denying the sadness he'd felt when the girl had looked at him, or the fear that had permeated the air when the Excursion had pulled to a stop and waited.

The man shrugged. "No idea. I walked over and said hi once. Back when they first started popping up here and there. Manager wanted me to go ask if she wanted a free meal. But it was mostly just to see what they were up to. Anyway, she hardly said a word. She declined the meal and offered to sell me a cold beverage."

Lance suddenly had many more questions. He started with the easiest: The mixing of pronouns the man had used. "You said 'they' just now. Who do you mean?"

"The girls."

"Girls?"

"Yeah."

"So there's more than one?"

"Oh, right. Yeah, I don't know how many exactly, but one day about ... damn, I guess it's been almost two years now, they were just here. Started showing up on intersections and camping out near some of the semi-busy touristy spots. All with their coolers, selling drinks and hardly saying a word to anyone."

Lance thought about this for a moment. Then, though he hated saying it this way, having to sound like a sexually excited teenager, asked, "Do they all look like her? You know ... hot?"

The man let out a rush of air, as though he were trying to calm himself down. Nodded. "Yeah, man. They're all smoke shows. At least for around here. Especially in the off-season, like now, when the beaches and bars aren't full of out-of-towners from the colleges that are close by."

"And nobody knows where they came from or why they're here?" Lance asked, feeling repetitive but finding the fact hard to believe.

The man shrugged, picked up the tiny ashtray and kicked the milk crate out of the way to head back inside. The sound of dishes clattering and grills sizzling intensified as he opened the door wider.

"I can't say nobody knows," he said. "And there's certainly rumors. The most recent being that they're actually Russian spies. But come on, man, this ain't Hollywood. We just know they're hot, and they're all over the place with their coolers. Look, my break's over."

Lance nodded. "Yeah, sure."

The man took a half-step inside, then stopped. Looked back to Lance and said, "Hey, none of my business really, but you look like you're..." He trailed off, trying to find the right words. "I mean, if you're looking for a job, I think we're hiring part-time. Cook and dishwasher."

Lance was about to ask what about his looks made it seem like he was in need of employment, but then remembered the sight of himself in the mirror at the bus station. He might as well have had DRIFTER written on his forehead. He needed a shower, and he needed to wash his clothes. He didn't think he smelled bad, but deodorant and toothpaste could only get you so far.

Lance nodded again. "Thanks. I'll think about it."

The man shrugged, as if it made no difference to him at all. "Pay's not great, and you go home smelling like you're deep-fried, but hey, it's better than killing yourself."

He waved a goodbye at Lance and was all but through the door before Lance shot a hand out and grabbed the utility door before it could slam closed. In his mind, he replayed the scene in the bus station men's room, with the janitor asking him if he was there to die. He remembered the hug from Barb and her reassurance that somebody loved him. He saw the watercolor heart on the flyer behind the diner's cash register. And now this: *It's better than killing yourself.*

"What do you mean by that?" Lance asked, and it must have been something in his eyes, something about his tone that suddenly set the man on the defensive.

He took a step back, positioning himself just inside the door, and said, "Oh hey, nothing man. It's just, you know, with what's going on here and all."

"No, I don't know," Lance said.

The man nodded. "Oh, right. Okay, yeah, you're new in town, sure." Then he poked his head out the door and lowered his voice a bit, like he was about to tell a secret. "Sugar Beach has been getting a bad rap lately. In fact, its new nickname is *Suicide Beach*. Young people keep coming here to kill themselves."

[5]

THE PIECES FELL INTO PLACE, LINING THEMSELVES UP IN A way that showed Lance a bit more of the picture. The janitor, Barb, the flyer with the heart and the number for the suicide hotline—Sugar Beach had a problem. Lance didn't want to know how many people had come to this forgotten little tourist spot to end their lives, but if he'd been in town for only a few hours and had already encountered this many references to the issue...

He had questions. Lots more. But after the young guy in the apron had divulged this last bit of information to Lance, he quickly repeated, "My break's over, man. Come back in later if you're looking for work." And then he pulled the utility door shut quickly.

Lance sighed. Walked back to the corner of the building and picked up his backpack and the to-go cup of coffee. The caffeine from his earlier cups had his head buzzing, but still he felt the grip of fatigue squeezing him tight. And with the overload of new information he'd just been given—the beverage-selling girls, and Sugar Beach's unfortunate nickname—he knew all at once that this was a business trip after all. Not a leisurely pit stop.

He was still going to eat crabs. The Universe would just have to deal with it.

He sipped the coffee, still hot. Took two long swallows and then headed across the parking lot, across the street, and then started walking down the sidewalk lining Sand Dollar Road. Toward all the hotels and businesses and the sound of country music still coming from somewhere.

The same direction the black Excursion had driven.

There were streetlights here, big and bright and casting artificial life across everything beneath their cones. Made storefronts and the entrances to motel lobbies look new and sparkly in the evening darkness. But Lance knew the trick. Come morning, when the sun was just rising and the light was dull gray and sleepy, the warts and wrinkles of these places would be exposed —peeling paint, chipped flooring, windows that needed washing, outdated furniture and dusty corners. New cars always looked best in the showroom. It wasn't till you got them home to your own garage that you saw them for what they really were.

He passed by two motels that looked as though they should be in hospice care, with empty swimming pools and a few beater cars in the lot. Doors to two rooms on the second floor were open, and the sounds of television echoed across the deserted cement pool area, down to the street.

The block ended, and Lance looked both ways before crossing the street. Once on the other side, Lance felt like he'd crossed more than just a road—perhaps a poverty line. A donut shop that looked clean and warm and might even sparkle in the daylight was on the corner, a few happy employees inside joking and cleaning up for the evening. Lance looked down to his to-go cup of coffee and briefly considered how good a donut would go along with it. Then he remembered his two slices of pie at the diner and decided to pass. Maybe he'd come back for breakfast. He made a note of the hours on the door and then moved on.

A pizza shop with plenty of indoor seating (Open). A surf shop with lots of t-shirts and trinkets and flip-flops and all the typical bric-a-brac (Closed). Two newer motels, side by side, that looked like places a family on a budget would come on vacation—not a Hilton, but leaps and bounds better than the ones a block earlier.

Across the street, the country music intensified, and Lance turned to see what he could only call a honky-tonk. Lots of wood on the outside and neon signs advertising beer in the windows. A set of antlers mounted above the door with a sign that read *The Sand Crab*. Lance thought it was a weird name for a country bar, but when the young couple pushed through the door, laughing and allowing the music to blare out into the street even louder, Lance saw the happiness on their faces and figured it didn't matter what a place was called.

Besides, he wasn't interested in the honky-tonk. In between the two motels was a wide parking lot serving both. A sign on the street told Lance there was beach access, free to guests, ten dollars a day to others.

Lance wasn't a motel guest, but he also wasn't going to park. Having a car didn't exactly fit his whole "traveling light" ideology. Despite his exhaustion, despite the way his head seemed to be foggy and his body begging for sleep, he felt a strong urge grow in his gut, his heart. He wanted to see the ocean. He looked down Sand Dollar Road, toward the rest of the lights and businesses and the cars parked along the street and the people milling about, and he knew there was more for him to see there, more to explore. But right now, there was only the idea of the waves and sand waiting for him to the east, an image that promised calmness and relaxation.

And something else. Though he wasn't sure what that something else would be.

He downed the rest of his coffee and tossed the empty cup into a trash bin by the entrance to the lobby of one of the motels. Then he walked down the side of the building, found the pass-through between the properties—a wooden bridge constructed first over grass and then rising higher as the ground bled into the sand. He stood at the precipice of the walkway and felt a strong, fresh breeze blow into his face. He licked his lips and tasted the faintest traces of salt, the grittiness of sand.

The moon was high above the water, big and bright and casting a shimmering gleam across the waves as they rolled slowly in and crashed against the shore. A lone lifeguard stand stood like a sentinel a few yards to the left, the wooden frame leaning slightly, warped and tired. Lance walked toward it, his sneakers feeling heavy and cumbersome as he trudged through the sand, yet he did not have the energy to stop and take them off. Felt the roughness of the grains invading inside, peppering the inside of his sole.

He climbed the lifeguard stand, feeling the sturdiness of the structure despite its weathered frame, and then set his backpack next to him and leaned back in the oversized seat. He felt he could fall asleep right there, and thought there were worse places to wake up than on a beach with the sun rising on the horizon.

But he had to do something first. He pulled his flip phone from his pocket and sent a text message to Marcus Johnston. *Still alive.*

Marcus responded almost immediately. *Good to hear. Let me know if otherwise. Be safe, friend.*

Lance used what little energy he had left to muster up a chuckle. Marcus Johnston, the mayor of his hometown and one of his oldest friends, had helped Lance and his mother on more occasions than Lance could count. Helped keep their secrets through the years, and had helped Lance the night his mother had died. He'd taken care of Lance's mother's affairs after her death, consulting with and keeping Lance in the loop the entire time. He hadn't had to do any of these things, but that was the sort of person Marcus Johnston was.

Lance owed the man a status update at the very least, even if it was vague and ambiguous. But the ambiguity wasn't only for Lance's protection. It was for Marcus's as well. Lance suspected the Reverend and the Surfer had gotten far away from Hillston after the night they'd killed Pamela Brody, and he knew they were actively hunting him, but that didn't mean they might not have other birds in the sky, soldiers doing grunt work in an effort to track Lance down. What means might they employ to get the information they wanted?

It was why Lance never gave away specifics.

It was why he'd been forced to leave Leah behind in Westhaven.

Lance thought of her now, imagining her here beside him in the oversized chair, her bundled inside a sweatshirt with their hands laced together and her head resting on his shoulder as they watched the waves crash. If Lance closed his eyes and tried hard, he could smell the scent of her shampoo.

He didn't know for how long he'd dozed off, but he woke with a start, his neck sore from the angle he'd been resting his head against the side of the wooden chair. He fumbled with his phone in his lap, thankful it hadn't fallen off and tumbled into the sand below, and saw it was nearly midnight.

The waves were still crashing, though the moon had shifted its position in the sky. The breeze carried the faintest sound of country music, still playing from the Sand Crab. Lance rubbed his eyes and rolled his neck and sighed. Debated just sleeping in the chair for the night, despite the chilliness that was creeping heavier into the air, versus trying to go check in to a motel.

And he just might have chosen the chair, if it wasn't for the flickering of light that caught his eye on the sand up the coast. A fire, impossible to tell how far away. Silhouettes of people huddled around, walking about. And at once, there was a growth of curiosity in him, wanting to know who these people were, if only just to see them. And, hey, if they were tourists—kids from the colleges that were close by, like the guy at the diner had alluded to—they had to be staying somewhere. Maybe they could recommend a clean motel.

Lance climbed down from the chair, shouldered his backpack, and began walking toward the flames.

[6]

IF IT WEREN'T FOR THE CHANGING LANDSCAPE OF
buildings to his left as he trudged up the coastline, Lance would
have thought he was trapped in some strange mirage, a trick of
the mind where, though he could feel the weight of his legs and
feet propelling him through the sand, he was unable to close the
gap between himself and the dancing light of the fire up ahead.

It was much further away than he'd originally guessed.

He would swear, in fact, that it had actually appeared *closer*
when he'd first set out from the lifeguard stand, and as he'd jour-
neyed toward it, it had continued to shrink in size, pulling away
from him step by step. Impossible to reach.

He was very tired.

The waves continued to crash to his right, the sound of the
ingress and egress methodical and soothing.

To his left, over the dunes and back toward what Lance
could only guess was still Sand Dollar Road, the businesses and
motels had become more and more sparse, larger gaps between
properties, either empty or filled with something hidden from
sight by the dunes. Then they'd stopped altogether and had
morphed into large beach houses. The type of three-story vaca-

tion homes you had to rent by the week and that were filled with an ungodly number of bedrooms and bathrooms. They had sprawling decks and porches. Lots of windows and balconies. Any number of opportunities to wake in the morning and view a sunrise that helped justify the rental fee. There were lights on in some, but others sat empty. Ghost houses until the tourist season started again.

Like the businesses and motels, these vacation homes eventually faded away too, replaced by smaller, more modest abodes. Lance didn't know if they were also for rent, of if they belonged to the actual residents of Sugar Beach. Most of them sat dark, but this could just as easily be because it was well past most folks' bedtime as it was because there was nobody inside.

The fire began to grow closer, the silhouettes of the few people around it becoming clearer.

Lance walked faster, feeling as though, if he could just make it to the flames, he could finally rest. Collapse on the sand if he needed to and sleep till morning, hopefully without a sand crab using one of his ears or nostrils as a new home.

There were five people in total. Four around the fire, sitting two by two on a couple of large, almost prehistoric-looking pieces of driftwood that were positioned around the bonfire. The fifth person stood further down the beach, toeing the line of the surf as it rolled in and out, staring out into the water and scanning the coastline as if waiting for a message in a bottle.

Lance's assumption had been correct—they did look like college-aged kids. The four on the pieces of driftwood—three boys, one girl—looked no more than nineteen or twenty from the short distance Lance stood. The person by the water— another girl, with long hair spilling down the back of her t-shirt —turned to head back toward the group, and when Lance caught sight of her face in the blue moonlight, she looked a bit older than the rest. Her face was more mature—wizened, even.

But not by much. Not enough to look out of place with the rest. A grad student maybe, working on something big, like a doctorate, perhaps.

She noticed Lance standing where he was, twenty or so yards away from the group, creepily stalking them. She didn't stop walking. Just offered a wave, which the rest of the group noticed and then all turned to look at Lance. Put on the spot, he smiled and waved back. The group looked curiously at him for another moment , then all turned back to the fire.

Lance wanted badly to go join them, to sit with some similar-aged people and just have a moment of relaxation and conversation by a fire on the beach. It seemed so normal—as normal as it could be for Lance. Normalcy, he found, was something he craved more and more as he got older. But he had no illusions that it would ever come. He'd accepted his responsibility to the Universe, and with his mother having given her life in order to allow him to continue serving this unseen, unknown agreement, normalcy was something he could only experience in small slices. Just like pie.

But he wouldn't join them. Not now. Something else had caught his eye. To his left, back toward the dunes, a single lamppost was planted in the sand next to the opening to a small trail leading back toward the road. A white sign fixed securely midway up the pole. Large black text. Lance took another glance toward the group, sighed, and walked zombielike toward the lamppost.

The sign read: PRIVATE BEACH ACCESS – BOUNDARY HOUSE B&B GUESTS ONLY.

A bed-and-breakfast.

Lance needed a bed.

In the morning, he would need breakfast.

And suddenly the lamppost felt like a beacon, a lighthouse on the coast that had been guiding him. He began to wonder if it had been the lamppost itself and not the bonfire that had tugged at his intuition to head this far down the shore. Calling him to the place that he should rest tonight.

He looked over his shoulder again to the group of college kids around the fire.

Or maybe it was both, he thought.

He headed up the path and over the dunes, in search of the Boundary House Bed & Breakfast.

[7]

THE CLIMB UP THE PATH AND OVER THE DUNES FELT LIKE the last leg of a marathon to Lance, but he pushed through, his legs burning and his backpack feeling like it was full of bowling balls on his shoulders. On the opposite side of the dunes, the land was flat and mostly empty, except for a large oak tree growing from the center of the grassy lot and four wooden benches set up around it, presumably shaded by the outstretched limbs of the tree when it was in full bloom. The walking path from the dunes made a wide circle around the outside of the benches and then continued on to the edge of the lot, where it met the corner of the sidewalk. Lance followed it there and stood, looking across the street at the Boundary House Bed & Breakfast.

It was a sprawling Victorian with overgrown shrubs and a stone stairway leading up from the sidewalk and through an opened wrought-iron gate. A fence surrounding the property was mostly hidden by the overgrowth. Lance wasn't certain, but even in the darkness, he thought the house looked as though it were purple.

A lone lamppost, identical to the one from the beach, was

just inside the open gate, another beacon guiding his way. It was, in fact, the only indication that the house across the street was the Boundary House at all. The only thing other than Lance's intuition, which he could feel practically pushing him into the road and across the asphalt. Thankfully, there was no traffic at this hour.

Lance crossed the road and took the stone steps carefully, through the gate and up to a wooden front porch complete with two porch swings, a plethora of potted plants, and a ceramic frog the size of a poodle that stared up at Lance with bulbous white eyes that looked like hardboiled eggs. The porch smelled of lilac and pine and soil. And something else that might have been mildew.

Lance nodded hello to the frog. "Evening, good sir. Might you have a room available?"

The frog did not reply, but a porch light burned next to the door, and Lance noticed a small sign mounted next to the doorbell that told him that guests could ring at any hour, which reminded him of just how late it was. Or how early it was, depending on your position on that sort of thing.

He didn't want to impose on anyone, and certainly didn't want to wake somebody, but as he was considering sleeping on one of the porch swings until an hour decent enough that he would be comfortable ringing the bell, he remembered the way he'd felt compelled to walk toward the fire, toward the lamppost.

He was supposed to be here.

Lance sighed, swallowed the anxious feeling in his stomach, and pressed the button for the doorbell.

Nothing happened.

No noise at all, not even a gentle buzz.

Lance pressed the button again, then again and again with the same result.

Then out of frustration, he peppered the bell with what

46

must have been thirty finger pokes and was working himself up into a maniacal laughter at his own silliness when suddenly lights flashed on inside the door. There was a not-so-subtle movement from the curtains covering a small window, a dead-bolt was thumbed back, and the door was pulled open with a force that told Lance the person standing inside was going to expect an explanation for his actions.

"Where's the fire?" the woman in the doorway asked. She stood barefoot and wrapped in a black silk robe with a swirling floral print, maybe a Japanese-style artwork. The material looked much too thin for the weather, but Lance figured it might have been grabbed blindly from a floor or closet, tossed on hurriedly to meet him at the door. She was tall and lean, with an athletic posture and an energy buzzing from her muscles despite her half-opened eyes and groggy voice. Her hair was shoulder-length and blond, with streaks of silver showing at the roots that betrayed her actual age. In the dim light from inside the foyer, at first glance Lance would have thought the woman to be in her thirties, but now he guessed she was likely at the upper end of her forties. It was impressive, to say the least.

But he had to remind himself he was on the verge of delir-ium. His observations and analysis should not be trusted at this time.

"Sorry?" Lance asked.

"The fire? There must be one, right? What with all the ringing."

The woman rubbed at her eyes, her fingernails painted a dark blue. Then she blinked hard two or three times and opened her eyes wide, as if taking Lance in for the very first time.

"Oh, yes, sorry about that, ma'am. I didn't hear any ringing, so I thought it might be broken."

"Do you know the definition of the word 'insanity'?"

Lance stared at her blankly, thinking it was much too late to delve into linguistics. He would need more coffee first. "I ... sorry, what?"

"The definition of 'insanity' is trying the same thing over and over again, yet expecting a different result."

Lance and the woman looked at each other from across the threshold for a moment, the woman looking as if she were coming more alive, and Lance feeling as though he were about to perform a forward trust fall into her arms.

Then she smiled. A thin, pretty smirk that made you feel at home.

Lance smiled back, his tired brain picking up on her humor in the situation.

She laughed, and ushered Lance inside. "Don't just stand there, come on inside." She stood to the side and waved for Lance to step in. He did so, first wiping his feet on a welcome mat outside the door and patting the ceramic frog on the head. "Good boy."

If the woman thought this strange, she didn't say as much. Only stood and waited for Lance's eyes to adjust and then said, "Welcome to the Boundary House. I'm guessing you need a room? Either that or you're here to rob me and I've just made things much easier for you. But I don't know that many burglars who start with the doorbell."

Lance smiled. Held up his hands innocently. "Not here to rob you, I promise. Yes, a room would be great, ma'am. And I'm sorry about the doorbell."

She waved him off. "Scared me is all. There's a switch upstairs I can turn on and off. I have it wired so that the doorbell will only buzz in my bedroom after I go to bed. That way it won't wake other guests if I get late travelers like yourself. Some kid from the vo-tech school did it. He's a magician with that sort of stuff, though I'm not sure he completely follows code all the time."

Lance's head was swimming, trying to keep up. The woman was talking a lot. He took in his surroundings, trying to get a sense of the space. He and the woman stood a mere two or three feet apart in a small foyer that was dominated by the staircase heading straight to the second floor. There was a green-and-red rug beneath their feet, atop hardwood flooring that was the color of chocolate, badly scratched and scarred and lived on. More plants here, sitting atop small tables and one hanging from a hook in the ceiling. A grandfather clock was against a side wall, near the entrance to what looked like a den or sitting room, the furniture looming in the shadows. Behind him, another darkened room with a large dining table and a fancy chandelier hanging above. A large wooden hutch full of plates and bowls and saucers stood in the corner, resting until the next meal was served.

The clock tick-tocked patiently during their silence.

"I'm Lance," was what he managed to say.

The woman stuck out her hand. "I'm Loraine," the woman said. "Loraine Linklatter. But everyone calls me Lori."

Lance smiled and shook the woman's hand. "Nice to meet you."

The image that exploded in his mind, the memory he'd pulled from Loraine Linklatter at the touch of her hand, nearly brought him to his knees. He gasped, then coughed, as if trying to cover it. Pass it off as nothing.

"Are you alright?" Loraine asked, startled, withdrawing her hand.

Lance coughed again for effect, then cleared his throat and smiled. "I'm so sorry. Been fighting a cold. Sometimes it sneaks up on me like that."

Loraine nodded, smiled politely. "Would you like some tea before I show you to your room? I've got a great decaffeinated lemon that's delicious. It'll help your throat."

Lance wasn't sure he even had the strength to bring a teacup to his mouth repeatedly without falling asleep, either dumping it on his lap and scalding his nether regions or landing nose-first in the cup and earning the world record for drowning in the smallest amount of liquid. Despite these thoughts, he smiled and nodded and told Loraine that lemon tea would be wonderful.

"Follow me," she said.

And as Lance followed the woman down a short hallway to the kitchen, he wanted nothing more than to reach out and hug her.

He wanted to tell her he was so sorry for her loss.

[8]

THE BOUNDARY HOUSE BED & BREAKFAST'S KITCHEN WAS clean and tidy and modern. Though it had the same wooden flooring in need of refinishing, and there was a small water stain on the ceiling above the sink, the fixtures and appliances were almost sparkling new. All stainless steel and metallic and out-of-place-looking among the rest of the older house. The refrigerator even had a large digital screen set into the door that was showing the current weather in Sugar Beach, as well as weekly calendar.

Loraine Linklatter filled an electronic kettle with water from an oversized sink and plugged it in. "Have a seat," she said, pointing toward a breakfast nook with bench seating at a small rectangular table.

Lance walked over and slid in, setting his backpack on the floor next to him.

"I know what you're thinking," Loraine said, pulling a ceramic mug down from a cabinet, then opening a drawer and selecting a bag of tea. She set both on the counter and turned to face him. "The kitchen looks like it belongs somewhere else, right? Not this run-down behemoth from fifty years ago."

"It's very nice," Lance said.

"Kitchens and bathrooms. Those are the two places people seem to care about the most in a home. No different for guests here, I've learned. I mean, sure, they like the bedroom to be comfortable and clean, but that's easy. But if you can wow them with the bathrooms and the kitchen, they're more likely to come back. At least that's my opinion."

Lance nodded. "It's very nice," he said again.

The teakettle began to whistle and Loraine quickly switched it off, pouring water into the mug and then opening the tea bag. She dunked the bag into the water once, twice, and then walked over and set the mug down on the table in front of Lance. He took it, thanking her, and began dunking the tea bag some more, watching the water turn a slightly darker shade as it seeped. Images of his mother sitting at their kitchen table doing this very same thing flooded his memory, and he couldn't suppress the small smile that came across his face. Loraine did not sit across from him in the breakfast nook. Instead, she retightened the sash of her robe—an action that caused Lance to look away out of politeness, not wanting to see something he shouldn't if there should suddenly be a gap in the fabric—and then she leaned back against the counter, crossed her feet and asked, "Just get into town?"

Lance sipped the tea. It was too hot and burned his mouth. Set the mug back down and nodded. "Yes, ma'am. Just this evening."

Loraine tried to do it discreetly—at least, that was the way Lance felt, but he sensed her taking in the sight of him, wondering about his story, why he was here. He was too tired to play twenty questions.

"Come from the bus station?" she asked.

Internally, Lance rolled his eyes. He really needed some clean clothes. Everybody was pegging him as a vagabond.

"Yes, ma'am."

Loraine nodded, and then waited, as if Lance might offer more. When Lance gave her nothing, just sat and sipped his tea and fantasized about the bed that was hopefully waiting for him up the stairs, she probed, "Did somebody suggest you stay here? Was it Barb?"

Lance shook his head. "No, ma'am. I found the place on my own. Saw the sign on the beach and just followed the path. I did meet Barb, though. She seemed very nice."

Loraine threw back her head and laughed. "She's a wild one, don't let her fool you." She laughed again and added, "But you're right. She's a sweetheart."

Lance finished his tea in three large gulps, desperate to end this conversation, not out of rudeness but necessity. As he followed Loraine up the creaking wooden stairs, her bare feet stepping exactly where they should after years of practice to avoid the groans and squeaks from the wood, Lance asked quietly, "Anyone else staying here tonight?"

At the top of the landing, Loraine turned and nodded. "An older couple from Bethesda, just passing through. They should be taking off tomorrow morning after breakfast."

Lance climbed the last three stairs, joined Loraine on the landing. "You haven't told me the nightly price. Do you want me to pay now?"

She waved a dismissive hand. "You're tired. Exhausted, actually, from the looks of it. We'll figure it out tomorrow. I trust you won't run off."

"Thank you," Lance said.

The upstairs of the house was square in design, the staircase poking its head up and creating a U-shaped floorplan with lots of doors. Three large windows behind, looking back toward the street, back toward the beach.

"Bathroom here, and there," Loraine said, pointing to one

door on each side of the hall. "You can have this room." She stepped to the right and opened the first door on the right side of the upstairs, reaching in blindly and switching on a light. "I'm straight back," she added, pointing toward the door in the center of the rear of the hall. "Knock if you need anything. I'm a light sleeper."

"Thank you," Lance said again.

"Goodnight, then."

"Goodnight."

Loraine headed toward her bedroom and Lance stepped into his, closing the door behind him.

After all the nights spent in cheap motels, naps in bus seats and, well, the nights spent in the *spook farm* back in Ripton's Grove, the bedroom Lance saw now was the equivalent of paradise. Plush carpet still fresh with tracks from the most recent vacuuming, with a large leather armchair in the far corner. A wooden end table with a reading lamp next to the chair along with a small bookshelf holding a number of hardback novels. A full-length mirror in the opposite corner, next to a closet with its door cracked open and an upright dresser whose surface was gleaming from a recent dusting. The air smelled of lemon and potpourri and, just like the front porch, the faintest whiff of mildew.

But the thing that had Lance most excited, the one object in the room that he would have gladly shelled out every last dollar he had for, was the king-sized bed centered against the wall, positioned below a wide window with thick blue drapes pulled shut. There was an army of pillows and the thickest, most inviting comforter he thought he'd ever seen. He hadn't brushed his teeth, and he hadn't used the restroom since the bus station —all that coffee was going to have to come out eventually—but he didn't care. He gambled that his teeth wouldn't rot out of his skull after one missed brushing and decided that he'd wait to answer nature's call when it actually rang.

He tossed his backpack into the armchair and kicked off his sneakers, peeled off his shorts and hoodie and t-shirt. Tossed half the pillows aside, spilling them onto the floor, and then pulled down the comforter and sheet and slid into the bed. Laid his head back and closed his eyes.

Lance didn't know if there was an actual heaven. Didn't know what waited for the spirits when they left this world. But right now, as far as Lance was concerned, this was the earthly equivalent. There was nowhere on the planet he'd rather be right now than in this bed.

He opened his eyes.

Maybe that most recent thought wasn't entirely true. There *was* somewhere else. Well ... *someone* else that would have made everything better.

Slurping at the bottommost dregs of fuel in his reserve tank, Lance had to practically kick his body into a sitting position to reach over and fumble with his shorts to find his cell phone. He pulled it free of his pocket and then repositioned himself back into the bed, wrapping himself tightly in the comforter and letting the pillow swallow his head. He used one hand to flip open the phone and click on his text messages. Found the contact he wanted and then used his thumb to peck out his message.

He pressed Send.

HER
(I)

The small studio apartment above one of Westhaven's three—yes, *three*—antique shops was nothing more than a square room with her bed in one corner, a tiny area that served as the living room, kitchenette along one wall, and a bathroom with a shower stall so narrow she had to monitor her carb intake just to make sure she could continue to bathe.

It wasn't much.

But for Leah, it was all she'd ever wanted.

It was hers.

After the motel had burned down, she had been certain her father would want to rebuild the place. It'd been in his family a long time, after all, and Sam was a prideful man. Who would he be without the motel? Without proudly telling everyone his daughter ran the place with great efficiency and professionalism, even though he'd never said as much to her?

Turns out, the fire was the best thing that'd ever happened to them. The insurance check was large—not win-the-lottery large, but might as well have been for a blue-collar paper mill employee who'd spent a lifetime living just on the upside of paycheck to paycheck. Her father had looked her in the eye two days later, as they'd stood together in the parking lot taking in the sight of the ruble and charred remains, and said, "We don't need this anymore, do we?"

She would always remember that look. How his eyes had looked softer and ... was it happiness? Relief? She would remember the way he'd looked at her because she hadn't seen him look at her that way since before her brother had disappeared.

That was when she knew they would be alright again.

All because of the night of the fire, and the boy who'd shown up and changed their lives forever.

Lance.

God, she missed him. Some people might think her silly for being so infatuated—*dare she say "in love"?*—with somebody she'd only gotten to know over the span of a handful of days, but Leah had never been one to care too much about what other people thought. From the first moment Lance had walked into the lobby of the motel, as she'd been behind the check-in counter after just finishing mopping the floor, she knew he was different. In some ways she didn't yet understand, but also in the best of ways. She could feel an energy, a connection between them. Despite all this, she'd still been surprised at how quickly she'd fallen for him. She'd see him again. She kept telling herself that. He'd had his reasons for leaving, and she had to respect them.

Leah lifted her arm and reached for her laptop's trackpad, clicking the NEXT EPISODE button on the Netflix page. She only had three episodes left of season two of *Stranger Things* and was wondering if she could stay awake long enough to power through. It was getting late, and she had the breakfast shift at the diner in the morning.

Just one more, she thought.

From her nightstand, a beautiful wooden table her father had built for her after she'd told him she was getting her own place, her iPhone's screen lit up and the speaker played a quick snippet of the *Ghostbusters* theme song, along with "*Who ya gonna call?*"

It was the alert tone she'd assigned to Lance.

A joke, she thought. Though she wasn't entirely certain he would find it funny.

Her face lit up and her heartbeat quickened and she rolled

over, nearly knocking her laptop off the bed to grab the phone. She unlocked it and read the message.

Are you awake?

She typed back: *I am. I may have an addiction to episodic science fiction thrillers. Translation: I'm binge-watching Stranger Things on Netflix even though I have to be at work in six hours.*

Lance: *What's that about?*

Leah had seen glimpses of this sort of thing from Lance in their brief time together, especially the outdated flip phone he carried with him and seemed perfectly content with. He was damaged, in a way. Although maybe that was too strong a word for it. It was more like he was out of tune with most of the current world. Pop culture things that Leah assumed everybody had at least heard of, Lance was honestly in the dark about. Oblivious.

Though she couldn't fault him. She had to assume she'd be a little out of tune with the world too if she spent so much of her time with one foot in another. She couldn't even begin to imagine what that might be like. Was so curious as to what Lance's childhood had been like, how a person was supposed to develop, or *be developed*, while they carried around with them such a secret, such an alternate way of life.

I think you'd like it, she typed. *It's about a group of young kids who have to fight off a supernatural evil to save their friend and their hometown. It's funny at times, and visually stunning. Sort of like you (wink).*

She would have used a winkface emoji instead, but she was afraid it might cause Lance's antique phone to crash.

Lance: *I know it's late and I'm exhausted, but I'm pretty sure you're flirting with me.*

Leah: *You're very smart, too!*

Lance: *I do try.*

There was a long break between messages then, and Leah wasn't sure if Lance had decided enough was enough, had fallen asleep, or was typing out a longer message that was made even more time-consuming because of his ancient phone without a proper keyboard. Her eyes were starting to get heavy, as well, and she closed the lid of her laptop, resigning to have to finish her show the next day. She was going to send one last message, a simple *Goodnight, I miss you*, but thought that might sound a little too much like boyfriend/girlfriend material. Not that she would have minded that, but she was still unsure what Lance and she actually were. His reaching out to her recently, after those first few weeks of radio silence, and the brief text conversations that had followed, had only further reignited the spark she felt for him. But this was a process she was going to have to let Lance lead.

But—and maybe this was the late-night version of herself talking, the inner voice we all have once it gets too late and we get too tired—that didn't mean she couldn't make a bit of a play. Give a little more effort.

She typed, *So where are you right now?*

She immediately wished she hadn't. Instantly felt as though she'd violated some unspoken agreement between the two of them.

A minute later, Lance answered, his words betraying his exhaustion: *cant tell u. But there smthing wrong here.*

All the happiness quickly deflated, giving way to a sinking feeling in her stomach as she read his words and flashed back to the danger he'd faced in Westhaven, then imagined infinitely worse scenarios. Hellish scenes that paraded through her mind as she scrambled to push them away.

She typed: *What's wrong? Are you going to try to fix it, like you did here?*

Leah waited a long time, but Lance did not answer.

[9]

LANCE DREAMED HE WAS BACK IN THE LIFEGUARD STAND, only the tide was higher than it should be, as if a great and powerful storm had recently blown through, and the waves were crashing all around him, reaching up to touch the dunes.

In the water, bodies floated facedown, swirling with the current and knocking into each other like bumper cars.

They weren't just bodies. They were him. Each of them wearing his backpack, strapped on tight and looking like a tortoiseshell as they floated.

It was strange, seeing himself from the back. Stranger still seeing his dead body—lots of his dead bodies—below him as he perched on the edge of the lifeguard stand and wondered if he should jump down. Wondered what would happen if he touched the water. Would he end like the rest of him? And then, in a blink, the water receded, the tide rolling out, and all that was left was five versions of his own body, lying stuck in the sand.

There was a sharp pain from below his stomach, and Lance's eyes shot open. He sat up fast in the bed, taking a moment to remember where he was. The armchair, the full-length mirror, the dresser, the bed—oh, the blessed bed. He remembered the walk on the beach and the tea with Loraine Linklatter, and then there was another stab of pain from his gut.

All that coffee.

Lance excavated himself from the sheets and comforter and crossed the room. He'd fallen asleep with the lights on, thankfully. Otherwise, he was certain he would have stubbed a toe or tripped on his own enormous sneakers and fallen on his face. He reached the door and opened it just a crack, peering out. The hallway was empty, which wasn't surprising given the hour, but from a room across the open space, he heard the faint buzz saw of a man snoring. The other couple staying here that Loraine had told him about. Lance took another quick glance around, saw nobody, and then walked on tiptoes in just his boxer shorts to the bathroom on his side of the hall.

The bathroom, like the kitchen, was top-notch. Elegant tile and fancy sink fixtures and a walk-in shower that Lance thought he could lie down in. The porcelain was so clean it was almost blinding as Lance relieved himself. He washed his hands, using a berry-scented soap from a foaming pump bottle, dried them on maybe the softest towel he'd ever felt, and then, after taking another quick peek in the hallway, made his way back to the room, closing his door on the buzz saw from across the hall. He switched off the lights using the switch by the door and then turned to head back toward the bed. He made it half a step before he stopped hard in his tracks.

There was a little girl sitting in the armchair by the bed.

She wore a blue dress with a matching bow in her blond hair. White leather shoes with a single strap. Six years old. Maybe seven. Lance wasn't great at guessing kids' ages. They all looked so tiny to him. The girl sat on the edge of the chair with her hands clasped in her lap and her feet crossed at the ankles.

She looked ready for church, or maybe picture day at school. But Lance knew the truth about her outfit.

It was the dress she'd been buried in.

Lance had seen this little girl before. Just a couple hours ago at the most, in the memory he'd been given when he'd shaken Loraine Linklatter's hand.

The little girl leaned forward a bit on the chair, looking at Lance expectantly. Lance stepped closer, walking around the front of the bed and sitting on the edge. Something hard jabbed him in the butt and he winced, leaning over and pulling something hard from beneath him. His cell phone.

Leah. Oh crap, I fell asleep. He tried to remember the conversation they'd had but couldn't. But that would have to wait. There was something more pressing to deal with now.

"Hi," Lance said. "I like your dress."

The little girl gave a shy smile, then almost yelled, "So you *can* see me!"

Lance chuckled. "I can. It's weird, right?"

"I thought you might be able to. I don't know why, but it was just a feeling in my tummy or something. Like, I knew as soon as you got here. But I didn't know if you were good or bad, so I watched you talk to Mommy and then decided you were good. You *are* good, right?"

Lance nodded. "I'm good. Promise."

"Mommy can't see me," the little girl said. But her words weren't sad, they were more matter-of-fact. Just telling the truth. The way kids do.

Lance shook his head. "No, I'm sure she can't. I don't think there are many people like me in the world. Maybe nobody else at all. You know, people who can see people like you."

"You mean dead people? I'm dead."

Lance Brody did not cry often in life. Hardly ever, in fact. But something about sitting across from this innocent little girl with her pretty blue dress and her sly smile and her cheerful voice, listening to her so casually announce that she was dead, not even aware of all the life she had been robbed of, all the joy and experiences and ... *all* of it, made a knot form in Lance's throat and caused his eyes to tingle. He swallowed hard and took a deep breath. Tried to keep his face happy and his tone casual.

"People like you," he said again. It was all he was willing to say.

"Well, I'm glad you're here, and I'm glad you can see me."

Lance smiled, big and genuine, and said exactly what he was feeling in that very moment. "I'm glad, too. Hey, what's your name, anyway?"

"I'm Daisy. Like the flower, *not* like the duck. Will you read me a bedtime story?"

"A bedtime ... wait, you don't sleep, do you?"

The girl laughed. "No, of course not, silly. I'm dead, remember?" She hopped off the chair, as if that was all the answer she needed, and pointed to the bookshelf with the rows of hardbacks. "You can just pick one of those. I don't care which."

Lance couldn't believe what was happening. He'd seen a lot of strange things in his life, and had done even more, but reading a bedtime story to the ghost of a little girl seemed so surreal and unexpected even he was having a hard time wrapping his head around it. But how could he ever say no? *Who* could ever say no?

"Sure," he said. "Why not?"

He stood and switched on the bedside lamp on the end table and then carefully stepped around the girl, scanning the spines of the books. He recognized a lot of the authors and tried to find a genre that was appropriate—at least as appropriate as he could get with the selection at hand—for a child. But then he started wondering if you had to follow the same rules of censorship when dealing with the *ghost* of a child. It wasn't like they could have nightmares. He didn't even know if they could really get scared. He marveled over how little he actually knew about any of this.

"You're really skinny," Daisy said.

Lance pulled a Harlan Coben mystery from the shelf and stood, remembering for the first time that he was nearly naked, standing there only in his boxer shorts.

"Yeah. Sorry," he said.

Daisy was now lying in the bed, next to Lance's own spot with the downturned covers. "Why are you sorry?"

"I ... uh ... I found a book. You ready?"

"Yeah!" Daisy laid her head back, her tiny skull half-disappearing into the pillow, and closed her eyes, a tiny grin on her lips.

Lance looked at her for a few seconds, fully aware of how much she now looked like a corpse, before sliding into the bed next to her.

Why?

That was the question he couldn't answer. Two different applications.

Why did this little girl have to die so young?

And the other question that Lance felt he would learn the answer to in time: Why was she here?

Lance opened the book and started to read, not being able to help himself and skipping the rare curse word. He made it to chapter three before he eventually looked over and saw Daisy was gone.

[10]

LANCE WOKE TO THE SOUND OF A DOOR SLAMMING SHUT.

He opened his eyes and sat up in the bed, immediately feeling more physically refreshed than he had in quite some time. The bed had been glorious, the comforter soft and warm, the pillow perfect. Lance had never been the type to lounge around in bed all day, even when he was in his early teens, but at right this moment, he glanced over to the novel on the nightstand and thought maybe today was the day he'd understand the appeal.

The novel.

Daisy.

He turned and looked at the other side of the bed and was not surprised to find her gone. Daisy had vanished while he'd been reading, but Lance would never forget the look of her as she'd lain there, silently enjoying him reading to her. It was heartbreaking, and Lance was glad he could offer her such a simple comfort, that short moment of pleasure.

He spied his phone, half swallowed by the comforter he'd thrown aside, and snatched it quickly, flipping it open and suddenly remembering that he'd fallen asleep during his and

Leah's conversation. Through a tedious and repetitive combination of button clicks, he went back through and read their exchange, smiling at the beginning as they'd flirted, getting that warm feeling in his chest, and then letting his face fall and his excitement dissipate as he'd read her last few questions: *So where are you right now?*

"Why did she ask that?" Lance asked the room, feeling a confused cocktail of emotions. On one hand, he was happy that she was interested, and curious as to whether she was trying to warm him up to the idea of her coming to visit him, maybe even travel with him. Lance wouldn't deny that he enjoyed the fantasy. But on the other hand, he thought she'd understood that her being with him right now just wasn't possible. It wasn't safe. Nor was her knowing his location. Maybe Lance was being overly cautious, but when it came to the Reverend and the Surfer, he didn't think so. Yes, there was a small part of him that was actually disappointed in Leah for asking. But he would shake it off. She just didn't fully understand. He couldn't blame her for that.

But he could blame himself for his answer: *cant tell u. But there smthing wrong here.*

First off, somebody call the spelling and grammar police. Apparently exhausted Lance should not be allowed to text.

But there smthing wrong here.

Second, he was no fool. Saying something like that would only cause Leah to worry. She'd seen and heard about what he'd been through in Westhaven, so she would understand that when something was wrong, and Lance tried to help, the odds of him putting himself in some sort of dangerous or precarious situation were basically guaranteed to be high.

With all the abilities the Universe had bestowed upon him, he often wondered why it hadn't thrown in some sort of physical superpower to sweeten the deal a bit. Protect their investment.

The ability to stop bullets would have been nice, but he would have also accepted invisibility or the ability to see through walls.

He was getting off track.

He clicked the button to compose a new message to Leah. Thought for a moment and then typed: *Sorry, fell asleep last night. First decent bed in a long time. I hope you have a great day!*

He sent the message, closed his phone, and then opened it a second later.

Not good enough, he thought. He owed her more than ignoring her question. Even if he couldn't tell all the details.

He typed: *You know I have to help when I can. Don't worry, I'll be careful.* Then he pecked out the same semicolon-and-parenthesis wink face that Leah had sent him the night before. ;)

He sent the message, grabbed his backpack, and went to take a shower before he set off for the donuts he'd promised himself the night before as he'd walked into town.

Just like the night's sleep, the shower experience was the best he'd had in a long time. Best he'd had ever, actually. The majority of the showers he'd taken in his life had been in the small bathroom he'd shared with his mother back in Hillston, the one with the showerhead that was positioned nearly chest-level for him, or the Hillston High School locker room. Luxury was something Lance Brody was severely unaccustomed to.

He could hear his mother now. *Why does a person need such a shower? What are they planning on doing in there? Do they get cleaner by having a prettier shower?*

Lance smiled at this thought as he toweled himself off. He pulled on clean boxers and socks, and then a pair of basketball shorts. He sniffed his hoodie and, accepting that it had exceeded its shelf life, added finding a washing machine to his to-do list for the day, if the Universe was willing to allow him that. He pulled on a long-sleeved t-shirt he'd picked up at his last stop— his last clean shirt, too—and then brushed his teeth before packing up his toiletries.

Back in his room, he made the bed and slipped on his shoes. He reached for the Harlan Coben novel on the nightstand, ready to slide it back onto the shelf, and then stopped himself. A feeling.

He left the book where it was, shouldered his backpack, and then headed out the door and down the steps, where he was instantly greeted with the smells of eggs, bacon, and biscuits.

And coffee.

There was definitely coffee.

He inhaled deeply, savoring the aroma. Good stuff, he bet. French press, maybe, or pour-over.

When he reached the bottom of the steps, he was greeted by the sounds of forks and knives on plates, along with softly mumbled conversation. He turned right, into the dining room, and found a couple seated at the table. They were on the far side of middle-aged, seated beside each other on one side of the table, plates full of food in front of them. When Lance entered the room, they stopped eating and talking and looked up, both smiling brightly.

"Good morning!" the woman said. She was on the shorter side, and while her features had gone a little soft with age, Lance could tell she'd once been very pretty. "Lori said you might come down. She just ran out to do her meditation but wanted us to tell you to help yourself to what's in the kitchen. She's just across the road in the little park if you need her."

"Thank you," Lance said. "I'm Lance, by the way."

The woman smiled and swallowed a sip of coffee. "I'm Melissa Keaton, but please, call me Mel." Then she reached and rubbed the man's shoulder. "This is my husband, Jon."

Jon Keaton gave a nod. "Hello, Lance. Come join us. We're about to hit the road after we eat, but we can chat for a bit."

Lance, never one to turn down food and coffee, and not wanting to seem rude to such nice people, nodded and then went into the kitchen. There was a small buffet set up along a long countertop, with just enough food for all of Lori Linklatter's guests, plus maybe two more people. This was a smart move on Lori's part, planning for more, considering Lance's appetite was considerably larger than your average person's.

He grabbed a plate from the stack and then loaded it up. Two scoops of everything. Two biscuits. And there, at the end of the counter, was a glass carafe of coffee with steam rising from the top in such a way Lance thought if he watched it closely enough, it might spell his name in the air, luring him closer. He filled a mug to the brim and then went to join the Keatons.

They did almost all of the talking while Lance ate and smiled and nodded politely. They seemed very much in love with each other—she always rubbing his back or tangling her fingers in the hair at the nape of his neck while they chatted, he giving her playful smiles and looks of ... well, they seemed very happy.

"Marriage is hard work, son," Jon said seemingly out of nowhere while Lance worked on his second biscuit. "In fact, we had a pretty rough time there for a while, but then..." He eyed his wife, locking gazes with her. "We went through something together that really opened our eyes. Best thing that ever happened to us. Taught us not to take each other for granted, you understand what I mean? You only get a few good ones in life, son. Cherish them."

Lance swallowed and thought seriously about what Jon Keaton had said. Thought of Leah. Thought of his mother. "Yes, sir," Lance said. "I think I do. I'll try to remember that."

The Keatons had to hit the road. They said their goodbyes

to Lance and went upstairs, returning a moment later, each carrying a small suitcase. They left out the front door, giving Lance one last wave and their best wishes, and then he was alone, the room suddenly very silent and very still.

His coffee cup was empty.

He sighed, stood from the table and took his dishes over to the sink. Then Lance grabbed his backpack and went out the front door. He was off to get his donut. The walk would help burn off some of the breakfast.

He also knew it was time to get to work. Even though, as usual, he had no idea what that meant, or where to start.

[11]

Lance stood on the front porch of the Boundary House Bed & Breakfast and looked out toward the road. Across the street, he could just barely make out the metallic shimmer of the water past the dunes as the sun perched high above. The air was cool, but the sun was warm. Winter would be here soon, and Lance figured he should savor a day like this.

He looked down to his right, greeted the ceramic frog. "Morning, sir. Fine weather we're having, wouldn't you agree?"

The frog said nothing, but Lance thought its face was in agreement.

He made his way down the stone steps and through the wrought-iron gate, and when he got to the corner of the sidewalk, he looked across the road and saw Loraine Linklatter sitting under the sprawling tree in the small park he'd walked through the night before. Her back was to him, and she was very still. *Her meditation*, Lance remembered the Keatons saying.

Lance didn't want to disturb the woman, but he also didn't want her to think he'd dined and dashed. He checked both ways for traffic and, finding none, walked briskly across the street, his body feeling strong and energized after the rest and a good shower.

There was a stiff breeze blowing off the water and overtop the dunes, and Lance was thankful for his long-sleeved t-shirt. He wasn't one to get cold often—hell, he wore shorts year-round —but a breeze could be an irritation if nothing else. He stepped over the curb and walked along the path until he reached the nearest bench, then he sat, figuring he'd enjoy the weather and the sound of the waves and maybe try his own moment of self-mediation until Loraine Linklatter was finished.

She was still facing away from him, sitting cross-legged on the ground, wearing yoga pants and a tight-fitting tank top. Beneath her was a faded blue blanket with white and yellow flowers.

Lance looked away, and then quickly looked back to the blanket.

Daisies

He felt an all-too-familiar twinge of sorrow and closed his eyes, breathing in the cool ocean air and trying to relax his mind.

It didn't work.

He had too many thoughts bouncing around. Too many questions he needed to ask, with no clue who to ask them of.

When he opened his eyes, he saw Loraine Linklatter had stood, her bare feet flat on the blanket while she bent at the torso, first leaning left, holding it for a few seconds, then leaning right and doing the same. "I'm about to start my yoga, Lance, so this would be a great time to tell me whatever you've come to tell me." She turned around to face him. "Unless you'd like to join me," she added.

"Um, no, thank you, ma'am. Flexibility isn't one of my strengths. I'd end up pulling something, and then you'd have to call the rescue squad to move me. Best for everyone if I decline."

She shrugged. "Alright."

"I really didn't want to bother you, but I wanted to make sure you knew I wasn't trying to run off without paying. I'm just headed into town for a while, but I'll be back. I can pay you now if you'd like. You know, if you don't trust me. I wouldn't blame you. I'm a stranger."

She waved him off. "I trust you. Call it a gut feeling. You ever get those?"

You have no idea.

"Yes, ma'am. I do."

"Okay, then. I'll see you back here later. Are you planning on staying another night at the Boundary House?"

"Yes, ma'am, if that's alright with you."

"Of course," Lori said. "This is the off-season. Plenty of room."

"Thank you, ma'am."

Lance wasn't sure when he'd decided that he would be spending another night at the Boundary House, but the words had tumbled out of his mouth before he could stop them, and he knew they were the truth. He wondered how many other truths he'd discover today.

Sensing the conversation was reaching its end, Loraine waved goodbye to Lance and started to turn back around, facing the dunes.

"I like your blanket," Lance blurted, surprising himself. He'd instantly understood the meaning behind the blanket, the flowers, but for some reason he wanted to hear it from Loraine Linklatter. Wanted to see what she'd tell him. "Daisies are one of my favorite flowers."

This was what you'd call a white lie. Lance didn't have any real interest in any flowers, but it was a tactic he thought might prove useful. He didn't know the specifics—did he ever?—but he was certain that the little girl he'd read a story to last night had more to do with him being here than she realized.

Lori turned back to him, glancing first down to the blanket beneath her feet and then back to Lance. She smiled, and Lance thought maybe it was the first *real* smile he'd seen from her. "They've always been my favorite," she said. "I named my daughter after them."

Lance nodded. "Very pretty," he said, holding back his questions. He didn't want to probe, didn't want to invade her memory. He'd accept only what she wished to offer him.

"She died," Loraine said, turning to look toward the dunes. A single seagull flew over the water, diving down out of sight and then quickly emerging again. "Cancer."

Lance swallowed. "I'm so sorry."

Loraine turned back to face him. "She was a fighter, though. Right till the end."

Lance nodded. What could he say?

Loraine Linklatter gave off a laugh that was half amazement and half frustration. "God, she was so beautiful."

Lance was quiet for a beat, letting Loraine compose herself. Then he said, "Just like the flower."

Loraine looked up at him. Nodded once. "Just like the flower."

Lance turned and started to walk toward the donut shop.

He walked past the *regular* houses he'd seen from the beach the night before, ones with secondhand cars in the driveway and the remnants of the spring and summer's landscaping still clinging to life. Houses that looked lived in, yet tired. Charming, yet full of history, and maybe secrets.

They reminded him of his own home back in Hillston, and a quick passing of memories washed through him and then vanished, like the scent of a woman's perfume as she walked by you. A momentary pleasure you couldn't quite latch onto.

After these houses came an expanse of two blocks that sat vacant and empty, the only signs of life the weeds and fescue that grew through the sand. It was clearly meant to be a dividing line between the residential homes and the sprawling vacation homes, segregating the work from the play, fantasy from reality.

Lance paid little attention to the homes. A quick glance here and there to shake his head at their enormity, their excess, and then he moved on, continuing down the sidewalk, heading back into the heart of Sand Dollar Road.

A donut waiting for him.

He'd made it one block past the last vacation home when the black Ford Excursion nosed its way to a stop sign from a side street to Lance's right.

The massive black SUV was like a mole on an otherwise unblemished patch of skin, its darkness a stark contrast to the bright sunlight and blue sky and colorful buildings waiting in the distance.

Lance kept walking, not wanting to stop and have it be noticed that he was staring.

Could be a different car, he thought. But he knew deep down it wasn't. This was the same vehicle that had picked up the girl with the piercing blue eyes from the corner outside the diner last night.

The SUV made a right turn without using a turn signal, and Lance wished there'd been one of Sugar Beach's finest in uniform parked nearby to see. If the Excursion had been pulled over, the driver would have to roll down the window. If the window was down, Lance could hopefully catch sight of a face.

Alas, the violation went unnoticed, and unless Lance planned on attempting a citizen's arrest, he was left with no choice except to walk fast and try to keep his eyes on the SUV.

It was impossible to do, even as the Excursion hit two stop-lights and waited its turn. Sand Dollar Road's traffic was moderate this morning, and as Lance got further down the strip, with its restaurants and shops and motels, he started having to dodge other people on the sidewalk as well. After only a few blocks, the SUV was only a black speck on the horizon, fading fast.

Lance sighed and continued his walk, mostly staring down at the sidewalk and thinking. That was one of the best parts about walking everywhere—it gave you a lot of time in your own head to think things through.

It took a lot longer than he'd expected to make it back to the Sand Crab, which was locked up and dark this morning, sleeping off its hangover while it waited for the party to start all over again tonight. He again marveled at how far he'd managed to walk last night after leaving the lifeguard stand, especially as exhausted as he'd been.

But this thought was quickly pushed away, because as he approached the donut shop, there on the corner of the intersection was a girl in sweatpants and a sweatshirt, sitting on a cooler and holding a cardboard sign.

The black Excursion was just pulling out of the donut shop's parking lot.

It was heading in Lance's direction.

[12]

THE SUN WAS NOT ON LANCE'S SIDE THIS MORNING, because when the Excursion drove past him, the glare on the windshield was perfectly positioned over the driver's side of the windshield, almost like when they blur out faces on TV to protect someone's identity. All Lance got through the wind- shield was a glimpse of an arm raised and then moving down, a to-go cup of coffee in hand. And then the SUV had moved on, headed the opposite direction.

Lance did not turn to watch it go, though he had a sudden longing to know where it parked itself at night, where its driver lived. He kicked himself for not trying to get a license plate number. Then maybe he could do like they did in books and TV, do some sort of research and find out who the car was regis- tered to.

But who did he have to call? Where would he look?

He sighed and walked across the donut shop's parking lot, beginning to think more and more that he needed a smartphone. Information at the tips of his fingers was something he was beginning to understand the value of now that he was constantly on the move, constantly presented with questions.

Plus, it might be nice to be able to take a picture of something that didn't always end up looking like a bigfoot sighting photo because of the poor camera quality.

He paused for a moment as he approached the door, standing to the side as a family of four walked out carrying a large box of donuts and laughing with each other—"Good morning," the mother said cheerfully to Lance—and watched as the girl on the opposite corner at the intersection stood from her cooler as the light changed, holding up her sign as a few cars lined up.

Her hair was blond and her face was striking, sharp angles and clear skin. And though the sweatpants and sweatshirt were baggy, you could tell she had a decent figure.

But this was not the same girl from the corner near the diner.

The light changed and the cars drove on and the girl returned to the cooler, casting a glance across the street and making brief eye contact with Lance before she sat down.

Lance went inside to get his donut.

And to watch the girl.

Inside, the shop smelled of dough and sugar and freshly brewed coffee, and despite Lance's large breakfast, his stomach made a noise that Lance recognized as its Feed Me voice. He ordered two chocolate glazed and a large coffee from a teenaged girl who looked half-asleep, yet was very polite, and took it all to a booth in the corner by the one of the front windows, sitting so he could look almost straight ahead and see the girl at the intersection.

He took a sip of coffee and a bite of donut. Both were very good.

From this angle, he could also read the girl's sign when she stood and held it for the oncoming traffic to see:

COLD DRINKS - $1
GOD BLESS

Lance had seen enough panhandlers in his life—yes, even Hillston had occasionally had spurts of drifters stopping by and begging for assistance, whether warranted or not—and one thing most of them had seemed to learn was that when you said GOD BLESS, you managed to play some people like a fiddle, instantly drawing sympathy. It was like a cheat code for beggars. And though Lance was certain some of these people were good and truly down on their luck and meant the words on their sign, he was also sure some of them were simply pandering to a group of people they felt would be most likely to give them something. God bless 'em.

Lance sat and ate his donuts and sipped his coffee and watched as the girl sat and stood, sat and stood, working each passing stream of cars.

Nobody rolled down a window. Nobody bought a drink.

After about fifteen minutes, a thought poked his way into Lance's brain and, though he hadn't really needed further emphasis of this, stirred that feeling that something was wrong.

It's almost winter, it's still morning, and the high temperature today will be lucky to hit fifty-five. Why sell cold drinks?

He thought about the SUV driving around picking up and dropping off the girls throughout the day. It was some sort of operation, dare he say *business*. But in doing some quick math in his head, he figured there'd have to be an army of girls selling a completely unrealistic number of drinks at a dollar a pop—especially at this time of year—to even begin to make some sort of profit.

His first thought was drugs. That would make the most sense.

But then a police cruiser pulled up to the red light and rolled down its window, a hand waving a dollar bill in the air.

The girl got up from the cooler, opened it, and pulled out a can of soda. Walked over and swapped it for the dollar. Then the window went back up, the girl returned to the cooler, and the police cruiser drove on.

Right into the donut shop's parking lot.

The officer parked, got out, and headed for the door.

He was carrying the soda can with him.

THE POLICE OFFICER WAS A BIG MAN, STANDING AT LEAST as tall as Lance and weighing somewhere in the ball park of three hundred pounds, and Lance could tell that most of it wasn't good weight. There might be some strength and power beneath it all, but Officer Soda Can was not setting any physical fitness records at the Sugar Beach station, Lance would bet his last donut on that.

He was middle-aged, maybe a bit older, similar to what Lance had guessed for Jon Keaton back at the Boundary House this morning during breakfast, and his hair was a sloppy gray mop atop his head. Big nose that looked as though it might have been broken a time or two, along with dark circles under his eyes and pasty skin that was shockingly pale for somebody who lived at the beach. His leather shoes squeaked as he walked across the floor to the counter, and the keys attached to his belt —along with the handcuffs, pepper spray and, yes, pistol— jingled along with each squeaky step.

His clutched the soda can in his right hand with fingers like sausages.

Sausages that could probably squeeze the life out of you without trying very hard.

"Morning, Mr. Tuttle," the sleepy-yet-polite girl behind the counter offered. "The usual this morning?"

Officer Tuttle offered a weak grin and nodded. "Yes, please, April. That would be great." Then he handed over a five-dollar bill and told April she could keep the change and waited while she handed over a tray with a single custard-filled donut and a large coffee.

While Lance was trying to figure out how a man Officer Tuttle's size only ordered one donut, while somebody Lance's size had ordered two—*after* eating a hearty breakfast—the man thanked April and squeaky-walked his way to a booth along the front wall of windows, a single empty booth separating him from Lance. He set everything down carefully, first the tray, and then his soda can, and then slid into the booth with a grunt and a sigh.

He ordered coffee, Lance thought. *He's got his soda right there and he ordered coffee.*

Either Officer Tuttle had a very strange idea for a new mixed drink, or he was only going to be drinking one of the beverages while he ate his donut and planned on saving the other for later.

But why bring the soda can in with him?

Lance swallowed the last bit of his second donut and then washed it down with a sip of coffee, watching Officer Tuttle's every move while trying not to be obvious, his eyes casually darting back and forth between the girl on the corner outside and the man in the booth in front of him.

Officer Tuttle sat facing Lance, but his eyes were downcast, staring at the table or his food or, very likely, Lance thought, his smartphone. He raised his enormous hand toward his mouth and shoveled in a bit of donut, chewed, and then wiped his face delicately with a paper napkin.

Another bite a moment later, his eyes still cast down. Then his head shifted slightly to the right, like he was noticing something different. It stayed there a while, then darted back to face in front of him. Back and forth a couple times, just as Lance had been doing, spying on the man and the girl outside.

If only I could see his hands, Lance wished. At the angle he was seated, with the backrests of the booths rising up high, blocking anything but the view of Officer Tuttle's chest and head, Lance was completely blind to what was happening on the table.

Finally, Officer Tuttle raised the cup of coffee into view and took a long sip, followed by another wipe of the mouth with the napkin.

Lance leaned back into the booth and sighed. It meant something, the fact that Officer Tuttle was drinking the coffee, yet had brought the soda can inside with him like some sort of pet. It was sitting right there on the table—though Lance couldn't see it—and not in the car, which meant ... what, exactly?

It means it's valuable, Lance thought. *It's more than just soda. He doesn't want it stolen ... or lost.*

Another follow-up thought, one that almost completely diminished the previous one: *But who would break into a police cruiser in broad daylight? He can't honestly think somebody would be able to steal it while he sits and watches from the window.*

Lance downed the rest of his coffee and looked out the window. The girl was up again, holding her sign for the row of stopped traffic, which was now more than just a couple cars. It had grown to a long line stretching far down the road. Traffic was picking up, growing dense. Lance closed his eyes and tried to remember what day it was, coming around to the idea that it might be Saturday.

Tourists, families, and couples were likely going to descend upon Sugar Beach on this, what might be one of the last nice days of the year before the cold really set in. Which would only complicate things for Lance. More people, more problems. He thought there might be a rap song about that.

After finishing off his donut and then gulping down the rest of his coffee in an astonishing chug-fest that brought to mind college fraternity hazing, Officer Tuttle looked as though he were about to stand from the booth. Lance, sensing his last moment to garner any additional information without having to flat out interrogate a police officer, lunged from the booth as casually as he could and took two quick strides forward, stopping in front of Officer Tuttle's booth. "Uh, hi. Sorry to bother you, Officer, but, uh, do you happen to have the time?"

Lance was sometimes so brilliant on his feet he felt the need to stop and pat himself on the back.

Officer Tuttle looked up at Lance with those very tired eyes, and then did a quick survey of Lance from head to toe—no doubt using his cop's intuition to assess what sort of person Lance might be and if there was an ulterior motive behind the question. Which there was, of course.

"Sure," Officer Tuttle said and pressed the home button on his smartphone (Lance had been correct on that point—the man had been looking at his phone while he ate) to light up the screen and display the time. While he waited, Lance stood there smiling and surveyed the table, looking past the trash from the donut and coffee, his gaze landing on the soda can. It sat upright, just to the right of the tray, unopened and boring. A generic brand of diet soda. Cheap and probably full of enough artificial ingredients to make a nutritionist blush.

It was just a soda can. Sitting there, like soda cans tend to do.

Officer Tuttle held up the phone so Lance could see the clock, and Lance nodded and said thanks and then went back to his booth, hearing the grunt and groan of Officer Tuttle as he extracted himself from the booth and then pushed out the door. Lance watched from the window as he got into the police cruiser, still gripping the soda can in his sausage fingers. Officer Tuttle cranked the engine, checked his mirrors, and then backed out of the parking space and drove away, heading down Sand Dollar Road.

Lance sat and thought, nearly laughing to himself as he realized he was trying to unravel a great mystery that seemed to revolve around a soda can. A lousy piece of aluminum filled with water and chemicals and artificial sugar.

But it was more than that. Had to be. He kept remembering the fear he'd seen in the girl's eyes the night before—those piercing blue eyes.

Drugs, Lance thought again. *It has to be drugs.* Though the thought definitely bothered him, considering he'd just seen a police officer purchase a can.

But with Officer Tuttle now out of the picture for the time being, Lance looked out the window at the girl on the cooler and knew what he had to do next.

[14]

LANCE WENT BACK TO THE COUNTER AND WAITED HIS TURN as a family with a toddler spent an excessive amount of time letting their child decide which type of donut it wanted. Common courtesy would have been to allow Lance to pass them while they debated, but they appeared to be too absorbed in the world of their child to notice other breathing humans around them.

The child finally decided on a plain glazed—*Really? All that time for a plain jane glazed?*—and the family moved on, carrying their food and drinks to the same booth Lance had sat in.

"Still hungry?" April asked. She seemed to have woken up some since Lance's first venture through the line, her eyes more alive and her voice more energized.

Lance patted his stomach. "It's tempting," he said. "They were very good. Coffee, too. But no, this is to-go." He placed his order, and April worked swiftly to fill a to-go cup with coffee and toss two donuts in a bag (one plain, one chocolate-covered glazed). Lance paid, thanked her, and then, just as he was about to turn and leave, he stopped.

"Hey," he said. "I know this might be a weird question, but what do you know about this place being called Suicide Beach?"

April made a face that told Lance his question had caught her by surprise, and not in the best of ways. He held up his free hand and tried to force a chuckle. "I know, I know, strange question from a stranger. But"—he shrugged—"I'm just passing through, and everywhere I go people seem to think I'm at risk to kill myself. What's up with that?" He tried to look relaxed, adjusting the straps of his backpack and then saying, "I just figured, you know, you're younger, closer to my age, probably. People like us tend to have a better understanding of what's really going on."

The girl was quiet. Picked up a towel and started to wipe down the top of the glass display cases that housed the donuts. Lance waited, sensing she was mulling over what she wanted to say. The door to the donut shop opened and a young couple walked in, holding hands and dressed as though it were eighty degrees outside. Lance figured he'd get along with them pretty well.

"Be with you in a just a sec," April greeted them and then turned to Lance, eyes pleading. "Promise me you're not really planning on killing yourself and just looking for ideas."

Lance, floored at the thought, again shocked at how serious Sugar Beach's suicide problem must be, used his free hand to draw an imaginary X across his heart. "I swear," he said. "In fact"—and here came the honesty—"I'd like to see if there's anything I can do to stop it."

He wasn't sure why he offered this last part, as he tended to usually draw as little attention to himself and his purpose as possible, but something about April's remark to him (*Promise me you're not really planning on killing yourself and just looking for ideas*) showed him that she was genuinely concerned, not just about him, but about the situation as a whole.

She was one of the good ones.

April gave him one last hard stare, then shrugged, as if it were nothing, after all. "I don't know much, but the rumor online is all these kids coming here, all these suicides, it's not random. There's more to it. It's not just the location that draws them, but ... there's talk that there's somebody here who's helping them."

Lance swallowed. "Helping them?"

April nodded. "Yeah, you know, like that doctor guy."

Lance thought for a moment. "You mean Kevorkian?"

"Yes!" April said. Then, "Hey, I gotta get back to work."

"Sure," Lance said. "Thanks."

April went to take the young couple's order, and Lance left the store, off to deliver the donuts and coffee he'd purchased.

As he walked across the parking lot, he replayed what April had told him. If there really was somebody in Sugar Beach assisting people with suicide, while it might be morally wrong, Lance didn't understand what role he was supposed to play in it.

Maybe I've got no role at all, he thought. *Maybe it's just a distraction.*

Instead, he'd focus on the girls selling cold drinks.

Lance paused and waited for a break in the traffic, a healthy stream of cars driving by with windows cracked, letting in the cool beach air. Smiles on the passengers' faces.

Because who didn't love a nice day at the beach?

As Lance used the crosswalk when the light changed, he suspected the girl selling the drinks hadn't had a nice day at the beach in quite some time.

He approached, slowly, and then waited while the blond

girl in the baggy sweats worked the line of cars, walking down the sidewalk six or seven cars deep before turning back around and returning to the cooler. When she started the trip back, her eyes fell on Lance and he saw the quick passing of her being first startled, then concerned, then the recognition, and then wary curiosity.

You could tell a lot from a person's eyes.

This girl's eyes were not the vibrant blue Lance had seen the night before—that sapphire spark that had penetrated the darkness—but they were blue, still. A deep shade that reminded Lance of royalty. The breeze blew her hair across her porcelain-like face, and she quickly whipped it out of the way and asked, "Cold drink?"

Again, that accent. Not as heavy here, but not quite hidden. She was younger than the girl from the night before, had to be. There was a youthfulness to her, an energy that hadn't been present with the other girl. Lance stared at her, analyzing every curve and line of her face. He looked deep into her eyes, and right then he would have wagered good money that if this girl was eighteen, it was only by a matter of days.

And despite the youthfulness, despite the energy, the sadness was still there. The wave of despair and frustration and loneliness that had wafted from the girl the night before and struck Lance in his gut. It was here, too. Though not as strong.

"Cold drink?" she asked again, repeating the phrase with a robotic frequency that was not inviting of conversation.

Lance switched off his detective mode and tried to turn on the charm. He held up the coffee cup and bag of donuts. "No, thanks. I actually brought you breakfast. Oh, well, maybe you've already eaten, but still. It can be a snack, then, for later. But you should probably drink the coffee now, if you want it. That way it doesn't get cold. I mean, come on, you can never have too much coffee, right?"

He was rambling and very much aware that he was saying a lot to say very little. But he couldn't help it. He didn't know where to start, couldn't quite crack the code to figure out what exactly he was trying to solve here. Let's say the girl was selling drugs. What was he to do? Say "Bad girl! Didn't you ever learn to just say no in school?" and then steal her cooler and run away like a madman?

Slow down, Lance. Take it easy for a minute.

He stopped and took a deep breath. Maybe it was all the coffee, maybe it was the growing sense of frustration of suddenly feeling thrust into two very different problems that he had very little understanding of, yet felt obligated to correct. He'd been on the go for what felt like a very long time now—one town and problem after another.

He was getting burnt out.

Or maybe you're getting lazy, he chastised himself.

He took another breath and looked at the girl. *Really* looked at her. Felt that sorrow again, despite the coy smile across the girl's fine lips.

Start with the girl, not the problem. You help people, remember? So start with people.

Lance set the bag of donuts and cup of coffee atop the cooler and stood. He stuck out his hand. "Let me start again," he said. "I'm Lance, your friendly delivery boy."

The girl looked at the food and coffee he'd set on her cooler and then looked up to him, using her hand to block the glare of the sun. She must have liked the cheesy grin he felt on his face, because her tight-lipped smirk morphed into a full-on laugh.

"Diana," she said, but she did not shake his hand.

Her eyes darted to the stoplight, and then she quickly turned and noticed the line of cars that had begun forming. The light had changed back to red, and Diana dutifully held up her sign and started the walk down the sidewalk. She made it six or seven cars deep, then turned and started back.

Nobody bought a drink.

When Diana made it back to the cooler, it was as if somewhere along the walk up and down the sidewalk, all the enthusiasm had been sucked out of her. Her eyes were no longer friendly, had turned back to business.

"You want soda?" she asked.

Lance thought about the way she'd so quickly reacted to realizing the light had changed back to red. Had seen that glimpse of fear cross her eyes and flood her face.

She thinks somebody's watching her, he thought. *She's afraid she'll get in trouble.*

This was definitely about more than soda.

"Sure," Lance said. "I'd love a soda." He pulled a dollar bill from his backpack and handed it to Diana.

"Diet?" she asked.

Lance shrugged. "Whatever you can grab first."

Diana's royal blue eyes narrowed, boring into him. "*Diet?*"

A flash of memory from inside the donut shop. Officer Tuttle with his can clutched in his sausage fingers. The image of the can sitting unopened on the table next to his tray as he'd eaten.

"Diet," Lance said. "Please."

Diana looked at him hard, as if trying to drill into him there was meaning behind what she was about to do. Then she gently set the coffee and donuts on the grass by the sidewalk and reached inside the cooler, pulling out an ice-cold diet soda and handing it to Lance.

Their hands met as she handed it over, and as Lance gripped the can, he gently held on to her fingers for just a moment, whispering against the breeze, "I'm staying at the Boundary House."

Diana looked at him with those serious eyes again, and Lance thought he saw understanding in them.

"I hope you have a great day," he said. Then he slid the soda can into his backpack and left, walking back down Sand Dollar Road in search of a coin laundry or some new clothes.

THEM
(II)

The Honda Element had been recently washed. The Surfer had said he'd liked the way the color sparkled in the sunlight because it reminded him of ocean waves, just before they crashed to the shore.

The Reverend was surprised, if not curious, at this bit of sentimentality from his partner—another mystery to add to the box of the Surfer's true being—but he did not deny him the task. Just like allowing the Surfer to pick their new vehicle, the car wash had been a concession that seemed a simple price to pay to keep him content. As long as the Reverend continued not to fully understand his partner's ability, he would not purposely dissuade him. They'd worked together well all this time, but friends they were not. They simply shared a common goal.

The two men sat in the booth by the window in the small diner that had appeared seemingly out of nowhere, nestled among short rows of run-down buildings on either side of the road. The only buildings they'd seen for miles, with the nearest town still several miles away. The diner, its exterior appearance, was quite modern and fresh on the inside. Fancy coffeemaker behind the counter and everything sparkling clean and up-to-date.

"Why here?" the Surfer asked, sipping a cup of coffee. "Seems, like, totally lacking in any vibes, man."

The Reverend heard his partner but ignored him. His gaze was transfixed on the building across the street, the one on the left end of the row. There was a wooden ramp leading up to the front of the shabby front entrance. Blinds drawn closed behind the windows. A single car was parked to the side, a small sedan that had nosed its way to the ramp's entryway, almost as if blocking one's way.

The Reverend had told the Surfer to exit the freeway and turn onto this rural highway over an hour ago—just one of those feelings, a pull toward something. The Surfer, now used to these sorts of instructions, having seen firsthand their accuracy, if not specificity, had not questioned the order. Had just silently reduced his speed and flipped on the Element's blinker and executed the maneuver.

But now, as the two men sat in silence in this lost but modern diner, he was asking.

Why here?

The waitress, who'd introduced herself as Rachel, came over to the table and broke the Reverend's thoughts. "You sure I can't get you gentlemen anything else today?"

The Reverend turned and smiled. His outfit almost always put people at ease, thinking that a man of the cloth would certainly mean them no harm or ill will. The smile—white teeth and an appearance of bashfulness—only sweetened the deal. He looked Rachel in the eyes and nodded toward the window. "What is that building behind me? The one with the car parked by the ramp."

Rachel's polite waitress grin faltered a moment. "Oh," she said. "Well, I guess it's nothing now."

"Now?" the Reverend pushed.

Rachel nodded. "It used to be Miss Sheila's place—still is, I guess. I mean, that's her car there. She still comes most days. But she doesn't run her business anymore. Not after what happened."

The Reverend waited patiently, his expression of curiosity unflinching.

Rachel took the bait. "She was a medium," she said. "She helped people communicate with their lost loved ones, stuff like that. Was super popular. I mean, people used to come from all over to see her. But then one day she just stopped."

"Stopped?"

Rachel nodded. "Yeah, I mean, she just stopped taking customers. Put a sign on the door that read 'retired,' and that was that."

"And nobody knows why she stopped?"

Rachel shook her head. "Nobody that I've talked to. Her assistant, Christina, came in one morning a few days after they closed up. She got a large cup of coffee to go, and then she drove off. Nobody's seen her since. So whatever decision Miss Sheila made, I'd say it's for good."

"How curious," the Reverend said, thinking to himself he had a very good idea of what had happened to cause this famous Miss Sheila to close up her shop.

More importantly, he thought he knew *who* had caused it.

The Reverend paid for their coffee and left Rachel a nice tip. He eyed the sedan parked across the street and said to the Surfer, "Come on. Let's take a walk."

Sheila Waugh—aka the famous Miss Sheila around these parts and for several surrounding counties—lifted her head from the round table covered in black cloth in the center of the room that had once been her main stage and tried to shake the grogginess from her head. Everything was fuzzy, as though she was coming out from under anesthesia, or just waking from the deepest and most restful of naps. She looked around the room, lit up more brightly than it had ever been when she'd sat here with the bereaved and put on her show, and then her eyes settled on the laptop in front of her, its screen gone dark. Asleep, just like she'd been. At least, she thought she'd been asleep.

She leaned back and closed her eyes and breathed in deeply, trying to clear her mind, regain her thoughts. She inhaled until her lungs were full and then counted to ten before slowly exhaling through her nose.

She remembered waking up this morning, alone in her bed, as usual. She remembered the quick bagel she'd eaten and two cups of coffee before she'd showered and dressed and then grabbed her purse and her laptop and headed here, making the drive she used to make with so much enthusiasm, so much antic-ipation of her performances. But now she came here, to the run-down office building she was stuck leasing for another three months before she'd be able to say goodbye and walk away from this place for good, with a different task at hand.

She'd decided, since she had nothing else to do and no other skill as far as she knew—she'd been Miss Sheila for so long, who was she without her?—to try her hand at writing a book. Fiction, of course. A ghost story. Because who better to write a best-selling ghost tale than a woman who'd spent the better part of her later years giving artificial voices to the dead, spinning tales and weaving untruths. Whatever it took to get the reaction from the paying customer.

Yes, she'd been here, writing a chapter that was going nowhere, when...

She'd seen them.

In her mind, she replayed the image of the two men emerging through the entryway from the antechamber, and she remembered thinking, *How did they get in? I know I locked the door.* An odd duo, looming in the shadow of the doorway before stepping into the light. One was dressed as a priest, she remem-bered, though she was not convinced he actually was one. She, better than most, knew how easy it was to deceive people. The other man—well, he looked as though he'd stepped straight out of a vintage beach advertisement, something promising lots of sun and sand and big waves.

But there was also something off about him, more so than the priest. She couldn't put her finger on it, but when the men had walked toward her table and stood on either side of her, she'd felt it, something cold and callous and ... terrifying. Whatever it'd been, it'd reached for her, and at the first inkling of it making contact, with a feeling of violation so strong she'd nearly vomited from shame, she'd opened her mouth to scream and the priest's hand had shot out and wrapped around her mouth.

"Shhhh, now," he'd said, his voice pleasant but his eyes dark. "Tell us about the boy."

And in an instant, she'd known who he'd meant. The image of the young man her mind conjured up was as fresh as wet paint.

With fear's icy hand still gripping her heart, she'd told them everything, sparing no detail.

"He ruined my business," she'd said when at last she'd finished her tale. Then, breathlessly, with a tiny, selfish feeling of hope bubbling up from inside her, "Are you going to stop him?"

And the next thing she remembered was waking up in the empty room, her laptop asleep and her novel unfinished.

15

LANCE FOUND A COIN LAUNDRY IN A SMALL SHOPPING center down a less populous road off the main strip. It was nestled between a pawn shop and a payday loan office, in case those who were waiting on their clothes to rinse and spin suddenly found themselves extremely short on cash. The sidewalk had been cracked and broken in spots on Lance's short walk, and he didn't need to look very far around him to realize that whatever glitz and glamour and appealing aesthetics Sugar Beach was clinging to, you didn't have to venture far from Sand Dollar Road for it all to start to fade away, the wrinkles and warts quickly exposed.

There was an overturned shopping cart next to the laundromat's door, along with one high-heeled shoe. Lance didn't want to know what situation had arisen that had resulted in both these items being left as they were. He hoped they'd belonged to different people.

He pushed through the door and was greeted by the smells of cheap detergent and bleach, the humming of dryers tumbling clothes and water trickling through pipes as it filled washers. The units were all old and beige, lining the entire left and rear walls and stopping hallway down the right wall to allow for a row of plastic chairs that looked like something you'd find in a police station interrogation room. (Lance would know, he'd been a guest of a few such rooms in his time.) The middle of the room held more rows of plastic chairs and some long tables for folding clothes. To his left, an ancient Coke machine rattled and sounded as if a wire were loose somewhere. A snack machine next, full of the standby classics: peanut butter crackers, M&Ms, chocolate cookies, and roasted peanuts for the slightly more health conscious.

There were three other people inside the place. Two women, maybe in their late twenties, early thirties, wearing pajama pants and sweatshirts, sat huddled together in chairs on the right wall, a small stack of magazines between them while they murmured conversation and flipped through pages, empty clothes baskets at their feet. They both gave Lance a quick look when he entered, then one girl leaned over and whispered something into the other girl's ear and they both burst out laughing, giving Lance another quick glance before returning to their magazines.

Lance had a mild suspicion the laughter was at his expense. He wondered if maybe he had donut on his face.

The other person in the laundromat that morning, Lance recognized immediately. Sitting in a chair in the middle of the room, leaning back with his feet kicked up on another chair he'd spun around in front of him, earbuds with a bright white cord snaking down to an iPhone in his lap, was the young guy in the apron who'd been smoking outside the diner last night.

Lance walked toward the guy, and when he was a few feet away, the man turned his head and his eyes flickered with recognition. He pulled the earbuds from his ears and let them fall to his lap. "Hey, man. Small world, huh?"

Lance nodded. "More like small *town*."

"Yeah." The guy shrugged. "I guess the odds aren't all that impossible we'd run into each other around here. What's up?"

Lance unslung his backpack from his shoulder and set it on one of the tables. "Even the lightest of travelers must occasionally wash their undies."

The guy smirked and made a sound through his nose that might have been a chuckle. Lance formed his small pile of clothes and hauled them to one of the washing machines, dumping them inside. He found the change machine and fed it some dollar bills, using the quarters to buy a pack of detergent from the dispenser, and then tossed this in with his clothes, thumbed quarters into the washer and started the cycle. He returned to the guy from the diner and took a seat next to him, leaving one empty chair between them.

"No work today?" Lance asked. The guy had not put his earbuds back in, so Lance didn't want to be rude. They were, after all, two dudes just hanging out in a laundromat. Might as well make the most of it. Besides, the guy had been fairly forthcoming with information the night before.

The guy shook his head. "Nah, man. I don't work Saturday mornings. They're too damn busy for me, even during the off-season. The servers love it because they make big-time tips, but us in the back ... it's hell. I've got some seniority, so the manager works with me. Grants me this one wish, if you will." Then, "Hey! Did you go see about a job? I checked last night after we met, just to make sure I wasn't feeding you a bunch of bullshit, and we're definitely looking for a part-time cook."

"Would I have to work Saturday morning?" Lance asked dryly.

"Uh, well ... you could ... maybe if you—"

"I'm kidding," Lance said. "I appreciate the offer, again, but I'm not looking for a job."

The guy made another noise through his nostrils that was

half laughter, half relief. "Nice. Yeah, it's cool, man. So ... what is it you do?"

Lance, not able to summon the energy to spin a white lie, said, "I help people."

The guy, to his credit, took this in stride, nodding as if he understood completely. "Odd jobs here and there? Whatever people need at the time?"

This time it was Lance's turn to chuckle. "Something like that," he said.

And then, from the corner of Lance's eye, he saw a flash of black appear. His head turned hard to the left, and through the glass window at the front of the building, he saw the Ford Excursion drive by, heading away from Sand Dollar Road.

Lance was on his feet in an instant, rushing to the door and out into the crumbling parking lot. To his right, the Excursion was maybe a hundred yards away, and Lance took off after it without thinking, his sneakers pounding the asphalt without waiting for any reason or justification from his brain. The only mission was to keep the SUV in sight.

I want to know where it goes, Lance finally processed. *I want to see what this person does when they're not playing chauffeur.*

But despite Lance's long stride and his athleticism and speed, two legs were no match for four wheels and an internal combustion engine. The Excursion pulled further ahead and then made a right turn down another street. Lance slowed, jogging to the stop sign where the Excursion had turned, and then he looked down the street.

It was gone.

He walked back to the laundromat feeling like a fool. Both for causing such a scene in the laundromat in front of everyone, and also for—he was now realizing—potentially drawing attention to himself from the driver of the SUV. One glance in the rearview and they would have seen him running after them. The same guy, they would realize, from last night near the diner, and this morning near the donut shop—if they'd noticed him then, that was.

Lance had caught his breath by the time he made his way back and pushed through the door, back into the aroma of bleach and stale M&Ms.

The guy from the diner was standing at one of the tables, folding several white t-shirts and stacking them neatly. He pulled out his earbuds and said to Lance, "Ice cream truck?"

It took Lance a moment, but when he got the joke, he laughed out loud, hard. It felt good.

He walked over to the guy and shook his head. "Sorry about that. I just ..."

What could he possibly say?

"You want to know where they live, don't you?"

Lance was stunned, and his face must have shown it.

The guy from the diner made that noise again through his nose. "You're not the first one, man. And you won't be the last. I mean, come on, a house full of hotties? What guy wouldn't want to see that? I gotta say, though, you don't really strike me as a stalker perv. So what gives?"

Lance considered this question. He could appreciate the certain look he was giving off by tracking down a house full of attractive young women, and what connotation it implied. He thought about backing off a bit, trying to step his way carefully out of the manure he'd stepped in and not leave more dirty footprints. But this might also be a moment where he could spread a little good around, put into a person's mind a willingness to help. This guy from the diner? Though he was reserved—despite his outgoing personality—Lance could feel the traces of honesty and sincerity beneath the surface. It was faint, but it was there, buried beneath hardship.

"Remember how I said I help people?" Lance asked.

The guy stopped folding his clothes and looked at Lance, readjusting his earbuds around his neck. They stood that way for a moment, the sounds of washers and dryers humming and spinning while the two men truly saw each other for the first time.

Finally, the guy asked, "Do they need help?"

Lance was honest. "I think so. But I don't know why. What about you?"

The guy didn't hesitate. "I think anybody who spends their days standing on a corner needs some sort of help. But even they might not know what it is."

Lance nodded, thinking it was a brilliant analysis of human behavior. "So, can you show me where they live?"

The guy sighed, gave Lance another look, and then nodded. "Yeah, I can. It's on my way home, so no big deal. Just don't do anything stupid, okay?"

That was something Lance certainly couldn't promise, but he kept this to himself.

16

"I'm Todd, by the way," the guy from the diner said as he and Lance stepped onto the sidewalk outside the laundromat.

"I'm Lance. Thanks again for doing this."

Todd waved his hand. "No big deal, man. Like I said, it's on my way home."

They'd waited until Lance's wash cycle had finished and he'd tossed his clothes into a dryer, thumbing more quarters in and starting the machine, which sputtered loudly to life and vibrated so much that Lance half expected the thing to start chasing them down the street. Todd, who'd finished his washing and drying for the day, had placed all his neatly folded clothes into a canvas duffle bag and then cinched it tight, slinging the strap over his shoulder and motioning for Lance to follow him.

They walked quietly together, Lance trying to figure out what exactly he hoped to gain by seeing where these young women were living, and suspecting Todd was trying to figure out whether he'd made a mistake in agreeing to show him.

"That night the manager sent me over to offer the girl that

free meal, I think ... I think I knew then there was something wrong," Todd said.

Lance kept his eyes forward, anticipating the black SUV to slide out from one of the side streets and roll up on them, somehow knowing exactly what Lance and his escort were up to, ready to stop them. He was being paranoid, he knew that. But being paranoid wasn't necessarily a bad thing, in Lance's experience.

"What made you think that?" Lance asked. "Did she say something?"

In his peripheral vision, Lance saw Todd shake his head. "Nah, man. Like I told you before, she hardly said a word that didn't sound like it was from a script. But ... well, you could tell she was skittish, for one. Scared, in that untrusting way a dog that's been abused gets, you know?"

Lance nodded. "Sure."

Todd pointed to a side street, and they made the turn together. "Plus ... and I'm not positive about this, because it was getting dark and the light was funny with the streetlight and the traffic light and all. But I think she had this bruise on her cheek, like, right below her eye. It looked a little puffy, and while I think she did a pretty good job of covering it with some makeup ... well, I think that's what I saw."

Lance felt something grow in his chest, an anger that he'd need to extinguish quickly. "And you don't think she fell down some stairs or walked into a door, do you?"

Todd sighed, as if he knew he was getting into a conversation that he'd tried to avoid for a long time now. "No," he said. "I don't think it was an accident." And then, after a long pause, "Now, that doesn't necessarily mean that whatever happened to her is happening to all these girls, or is even remotely related to whatever it is they're actually doing out there on the street—because, let's face it, you and I both know there's more going on here than just selling knock-off-brand soda. Maybe she's got a boyfriend who got pissy one night, or one of the other girls slugged her because she ate her Lean Cuisine or some shit like that. I mean, catfights can get vicious, man, you know?"

Lance said nothing, letting Todd finish his rambling.

"But I guess it's just a feeling I got, man. The way she looked at me, and the way that bruise seemed to stand out on her face." He shrugged and shook his head. "I guess from that night on, I always had this little idea that while I probably wouldn't condone whatever it is they were doing, nobody deserves to get abused."

Lance thought for a bit as they walked. The houses along this street were nicer, well kept. Most had freshly painted shutters and lawns that still looked respectable despite the weather. Newer-model cars in driveways. Basketball hoops here and there. The sound of the rubber ball bouncing on asphalt causing Lance's head to swing to the left, where he found two teenage boys playing a game of HORSE. It'd been a long time since he'd shot a ball. He found that he was starting to crave it.

Soon, he thought. *The next chance I get.*

Lance cleared his throat and brought his thoughts back to the present. "I've always liked the word *condone*," he said.

Todd turned and looked at him. "What?"

"You said you probably wouldn't condone whatever it is the girls are doing. I'm just saying I've always liked that word … condone." He shrugged. "It just sounds good, and it's fun to say."

Todd made that noise through his nose again. "You were a dork in high school, weren't you?"

Lance made a maybe/maybe not gesture with his hand, then said, "All-State basketball, four years in a row. But I also read a lot."

Todd nodded. "Nice combo." Then he pointed to the left when they'd reached another intersection. "This way."

They crossed the street and Lance nodded toward the nicer homes that surrounded them. "You live in a house like this?"

Todd shook his head. "Yeah, on my part-time diner cook's wages, I can afford a single-family home with a yard, yet every Saturday morning, I still walk all this way to the nearest coin laundry, where I've chosen to lounge for two hours."

"Point taken," Lance said, sensing Todd's sarcasm for what it truly was. A deflection. A defense against his truth.

"I rent one half a duplex with two other dudes. I mean, don't get me wrong, it's not a shithole or anything, but this"—he nodded to the neighborhood—"this only goes another couple blocks, then you're right back into minimum-wage-ville."

Lance stopped walking, his sneakers nearly skidding on the sidewalk. Todd turned to look at him and then followed Lance's gaze across the street. Then recognition set in.

"That's it, isn't it?" Lance asked, staring at the house.

"How in the *hell* did you know that?" Todd said, ignoring the house and looking directly at Lance.

Lance heard the question, but he had no answer. Not one that wouldn't create even more suspicion. He'd opened up to Todd as much as he was willing to for now, and what he'd told the guy, while it wasn't exactly a lie—he *was* here to help these girls, if he could—it certainly was nowhere near the entire truth.

So he just walked away, crossing the residential street with a casualness that suggested he knew exactly where he was going, leaving Todd confused on the sidewalk. Halfway across the road, Lance heard footsteps behind him as Todd jogged to catch up.

The house was a two-story brick colonial with bright white trim. Sharp lines and crisp color. The yard was neat and tidy and looked healthy, taken care of. Flowerbeds ran along the front of the house, filled with white rock and looking just as fresh as spring. There was a white privacy fence protecting the backyard. A gate on the right side of the house, shut and likely locked. The driveway was the dark black of a recent seal job, feeding into an attached two-car garage. The garage door was closed, but Lance knew exactly what was behind it: a black Ford Excursion, engine still warm.

The house looked completely ordinary. Was, in fact, a picture-perfect suburban family home. If you closed your eyes, you'd be able to hear the squeals of children running through backyard sprinklers in the summer, smell the wafting aroma of meat cooking on a grill while music played from outdoor speakers and husband and wife gave each other a playful kiss and longing look and then laughed and marveled at this little slice of heaven they'd built.

The house looked completely ordinary, except for two things.

First, the cameras. They were small and unobtrusive and blended well if you weren't looking for them, but Lance picked them out immediately. There was one near the front door, and two more on each corner of the house. Wide-angle lenses, more than likely, to capture the maximum amount of picture with the least amount of hardware. Lance suspected that with those three cameras alone, the owners had a clear view of the entire front and both sides of the home. Not unusual, if not a bit extreme. Home security was a big deal to a lot of people.

But the second thing that made the house less than ordinary to Lance, the thing that couldn't be seen from the street or heard from the backyard, was the sadness he felt. The same feeling he'd gotten both times he'd approached the girls with the coolers. It was here, living, breathing, growing. This was the source. If not directly, it was housed here. A lot of it. Enough that, if

Lance had not spent his life dealing with such things, it might have brought him to tears.

Lance stood silently on the corner and looked at the house for another few seconds before the unease began to creep in. "We should go," he said.

"Yeah," Todd agreed. "I need to get home. Gonna catch a few winks before work tonight. You good?"

Lance nodded, keeping his eyes on the house. "I'm good. Thanks again."

Todd was halfway turned to leave when he stopped. "Hey, you got a phone?"

"I do."

"Let me give you my number. You know, in case you need to ... I don't know, place a to-go order or something." He made that noise through his nostrils again. Lance agreed and pulled out his phone, punching in Todd's number.

"Cool, man. I'll see you around. Take care," Todd said, and then he was off, down to the end of the block and around the corner, disappearing down another street.

Getting what he'd come for, and with no other plan in mind, Lance took one last look at the house and then headed back to get his clothes from the laundromat.

As he walked, he thought about the cameras and the big privacy fence, coupled with the deep, undeniable feeling of sadness.

They're not keeping people out, Lance thought. *They're keeping people in.*

17

NOBODY HAD STOLEN HIS CLOTHES FROM THE DRYER, which was good. He liked his hoodie and his shorts, and so far they'd served him well. He could always buy more underwear and socks, but what an unnecessary hassle that would have been. The girls with the magazines had left by the time he returned, and in their place was an elderly woman who looked brittle enough to snap in two, but had lifted her overflowing clothes basket up onto the table with such ease that Lance figured she might have a future hustling people in arm-wrestling matches down at the Sand Crab.

She smiled at Lance as he left, and he wished her a good day.

He found a submarine sandwich shop on the strip and ordered a turkey on wheat, extra meat, loading it up with lots of vegetables and a single squirt of mayo for a little flavor. He got it to go, thinking he'd take it back to the little park across from the Boundary House and have a picnic with himself. The weather was still perfect, even warmer now that the sun had reached its peak, and considering it was only lunchtime, he'd done a lot and found himself with a lot to think about.

As he made his way, leaving the busiest of the traffic behind, he heard the sounds from the beach over the dunes. People shouting and laughing, the *thud ... thud ... thud* of what might have been a volleyball game, and of course, the waves crashing. An ever-present accompaniment to the sounds of life and fun on the sand.

He thought about the kids he'd seen on the beach the night before. Wondered if they were out there now, or if they only emerged at night to enjoy the fire.

Two of the enormous rental houses had cars in the drive-ways: crew-cab trucks and SUVs, people-moving vehicles. Families who'd set out to enjoy themselves and didn't mind paying for it. Lance wondered what that feeling must be like, questioning whether it was something he'd ever get to experience. And for not the first time, he wondered just what future the Universe had planned for him. Was this it? Forever the servant, on the move helping to fix things here and there and everywhere until the day he died?

He thought of Leah.

I hope there's more to me than that.

He thought of his mother. Her sacrifice.

But I'll have to accept it if there isn't.

Ahead, the Boundary House came into view and so did the little park opposite, which sat empty and waiting. He was maybe twenty yards away when Loraine Linklatter called to him, standing from one of the Boundary House's porch swings and walking to the stoop.

"Oh good, I was hoping you'd make it back in time! I was just about to set out lunch."

Lance smiled but cast a look to the park, feeling the weight of his sub in his backpack. "That's very kind of you, but I was just going to eat a sandwich I bought."

Loraine Linklatter didn't like this. "Sandwich? *Please*. Get up here now. You won't regret it."

Lance sighed. He was technically paying for his room and board at the Boundary House, though he had been unaware that included lunch.

"Save the sandwich for dinner," Loraine called out. "I made crab salad."

Lance sighed and started walking toward the house. He had promised himself he was going to eat crabs while he was in Sugar Beach, though this wasn't exactly what he had in mind.

Loraine Linklatter had traded her yoga pants and tank top for a pair of tight-fitting jeans and a light cream sweater, the sleeves pushed up around her elbows, her feet still bare. Lance was beginning to wonder if she ever wore shoes, if this was some sort of beach lifestyle trait. She'd showered since the morning yoga, and her hair shined in the sunlight and curled naturally around her face. The tiniest bit of makeup, but nothing extravagant. Lance again found himself impressed with how her actual age seemed a mystery. *Maybe I should start doing yoga*, he thought.

"Did you do some sightseeing this morning?" Loraine asked, welcoming Lance up onto the porch and then inside the house.

"I did laundry," Lance said.

Loraine whipped her head around as she walked down the hall toward the kitchen. "*Laundry?* You didn't have to go out and do that. You certainly could have used the washer and dryer here. You should have asked me."

Lance, while he was glad for his laundromat trip because it had led him to Todd and the location of the soda girls' home, feigned his own ignorance about considering being able to wash his clothes here and nodded his head, saying that was very kind of her to offer. Looking back, he wondered why, in fact, he hadn't considered asking. The obvious answer was the Universe hadn't wanted him to. Lance sometimes hated moments like this, the moments where it felt like he was nothing but a puppet. But it also added to the fact that he felt his meeting Todd and learning more about the girls were all part of whatever plan was at work here.

In the kitchen, all signs of breakfast were gone. Only sparkling clean countertops and an empty sink remained. Not even a single pot or pan in the drying rack. Loraine walked to the fancy refrigerator and swung the door open wide, removing a large stainless-steel bowl covered in plastic wrap. She pulled two small ceramic bowls down from a cabinet and, using a large spoon from one of the drawers, scooped a heaping pile of crab salad into one and handed it to Lance.

"Go," she said, nodding toward the breakfast nook, "sit."

Lance obeyed and watched as Loraine scooped her own helping into a bowl and then grabbed a box of crackers from the pantry and two forks from a drawer and brought it all over to the table, setting them down and asking, "Drink? I've got iced tea, lemonade, water..."

"Water is fine, thank you, ma'am."

She pulled a filtered pitcher from the fridge and filled two glasses, returning to the table and sliding into the seat opposite Lance.

"Well, dig in," she said, opening a sleeve of crackers and selecting one, using her fork to pile a scoop of crab salad onto it before popping it into her mouth. Lance, unfamiliar with what he was about to eat or how to go about doing so, followed her lead and tried the same thing.

It was delicious, and he quickly set to it, nearly polishing off an entire sleeve of crackers on his own. Loraine was eating much slower, and as Lance was finishing his bowl, he noticed her watching him, almost as if she were studying him.

He swallowed and said, "Do I have stuff on my face? It's not donut, is it?"

Loraine smiled, all lips, no teeth, almost pitying. Lance sat back, meeting her stare. He tried to smile, too.

"Ma'am?" he asked.

Loraine Linklatter took a sip of water and set the glass back on the table. The way the light came through the window in the breakfast nook, her face was lit up like she was about to have her portrait taken, and in that warm bath of sunlight, Lance could see some of the years melt away from her face. What he saw there was jarring, because it was no longer Loraine Linklatter's face he saw, but a teenaged version of herself. And *that* face, Lance thought, looked less like a young Loraine than it did an *older* Daisy.

Something about that girl, Lance had time to think, before Loraine asked, "So, Lance. What's your story?"

Lance felt something coil inside him. Something protective and hesitant. It was a familiar feeling. One he'd experienced all his life. His story, if you will, was almost never one he could tell.

"Story?" he asked, grabbing another cracker and chewing it.

"Yes!" Loraine said cheerfully. "Who are you, where are you from, where are you going? I love hearing about my guests. At this point in my life, I tend to live vicariously through those I meet, if you know what I mean."

Lance shrugged. "I'm Lance, and I'm just passing through." He smiled as he said this, trying to imply that he was not trying to be a smart-ass, but simply asking that she respect his privacy. Surely not every guest of the Boundary House spilled their entire life story to a woman they didn't know.

"Where are you passing through to?" Loraine asked, apparently not falling for Lance's subterfuge. "Headed back home, or further away?"

Lance, thinking if he was vague enough, or maybe mysterious enough, Loraine might drop the subject, said, "Sometimes both. I never know, really."

Loraine just pushed on, lifting her bowl and scooping up the last few bites of her crab salad. "Got a girlfriend somewhere? Wife? Partner?"

"No." Despite what he and Leah might be, he would not be presumptuous, especially not with someone who was essentially a stranger. He felt the coil tighten more inside him.

"Surprising," Loraine said. "Good-looking guy like yourself." Then she added, "What about family? Mom, dad ... siblings?"

Lance took a slow breath, steadying his nerve. "No," he said coolly. Then, tired of the interrogation, he decided to flip things, ask his own question. "What about you? Do you have a boyfriend, husband, partner? Do you live here alone?"

And it was as if somebody had sucked the air out of the room. Loraine didn't so much have a physical reaction to the question, as she had no reaction at all. They sat there across the table from each other for a few quiet seconds before Loraine grabbed both of their empty bowls and carried them to the sink.

"I hope you enjoyed lunch," she said. "Now if you'll excuse me, I have some things to do."

Lance stood from the table. "Of course. Thank you." Then, as he picked up his backpack, he asked, "Do you mind if I put my sub in the fridge?"

Loraine said nothing, but Lance saw a tiny nod as she began washing the bowls by hand.

"Thank you," Lance said, pulling his sandwich from his backpack and finding a place for it inside the enormous refrigerator. Then he headed up the stairs, wanting to be anywhere except the kitchen.

———

Loraine Linklatter had made his bed, tucking the sheets tight and restacking the pile of pillows in the same artsy way they'd been the night before, but otherwise the room looked the same, including, Lance saw, the Harlan Coben novel still sitting on the nightstand.

Lance walked to the side of the bed and kicked off his shoes, lying down with his back propped against the army of pillows. Took a deep breath.

He felt a small bit of regret at using the question about Loraine Linklatter's husband as his escape from her attempted inquisition into his life. It was a low blow, he told himself. He'd gotten frustrated and had started to shut down, as he sometimes found himself doing when he considered his past. His secrets were too big, and the wound left by the loss of his mother was still too fresh.

But he was better than that, he scolded himself. *You hurt her on purpose to protect yourself.*

When Lance had shaken Loraine Linklatter's hand last night, he'd received one of his instant downloads, as he liked to call them: a heartbreaking montage of rapid-fire memories pulled from Loraine's mind, her past. He'd seen Daisy, when she was alive and happy and full of life, and then had bounced along the timeline from the first day she'd told Lori she didn't feel well, to the test and diagnosis, and then the end. There were holes in the timeline—days, weeks, and even months sometimes between scenes—but the final image, Loraine Linklatter standing graveside, watching as her little girl's casket was lowered into the earth, was the only one Lance felt really mattered. It was the definitive moment. The one that Loraine herself could not seem to shake from her mind, as if it haunted her.

But in these images, there was another cast member in the film. Standing beside Loraine in the doctor's office, at Daisy's bedside, and also in the cemetery on that day, was a man. Lance did not know his name, but he knew his role: father and husband.

Loraine Linklatter had been married, and now, it seemed, she wasn't.

Lance didn't know what had happened to the man, but judging from Loraine's reaction to his question in the kitchen, the circumstances had not been good.

And somehow, Lance had known this. He didn't know the details, but he'd known when he'd formed the question on his lips and tossed it to Loraine across the table that it was going to hit her hard. And it had.

That's not you, Lance. *You're better than that.*

He sighed, needing to move on from the moment and put his mind to use for something else. He pulled his backpack up off the floor and onto the bed with him, unzipping it and retrieving the soda can he'd bought from the girl near the donut shop. He tossed his bag back onto the floor, held the can up into the light spilling through the window blinds behind him.

"Okay," he said to the can, "let's see if we can figure out what you really are."

[18]

THE OUTSIDE OF THE SODA CAN WAS ... WELL, EXACTLY LIKE the outside of soda can should be: aluminum, cylindrical, ripe with pressure from the carbonated liquid inside. The printing of the words and the logo for the generic brand of diet soda all looked normal, despite Lance's best efforts at combing through each and every line of text—including all the ingredients!—in search of some sort of hidden message. He found nothing. He even tried to unscrew the bottom of the can, thinking of that guy in *Jurassic Park* smuggling the dinosaur DNA in the bottom of a can of shaving cream.

The bottom of the can did not twist off, nor did the top. There was no wrapper to peel off, potentially revealing something underneath. The can looked normal.

Which means whatever was so important must be on the inside.

Lance thought again about drugs, having to convince himself that having seen a police officer purchase a can of the stuff earlier did not necessarily negate any possible scenario.

Crooked cops were not unheard of. Cops with addictions

either. Everyone gets down and out sometimes, and not everyone handles it in the best way.

Lance looked at the can in his hand and knew what he had to do. He got up from the bed and peeked his head out the door, seeing and hearing nobody. Then he padded down to the luxurious bathroom and closed and locked the door behind him. Standing over the sink, he popped the tab of the soda, that *pshhhhh* sound of the air escaping the can sounding very loud in the stillness of the room. He held the can to his ear and listened to the fizzing inside, sniffed the opening and smelled...

Soda. Nothing but diet soda.

He poured some out, into the sink. Watched it swirl down the drain. It didn't look radioactive. It looked like soda.

He sighed. The next and final test was the one he was more concerned about. Lance had never ingested any illegal substances—nor, really, any diet soda. His mother had always been very against sodas—but he knew the only way he could allow himself to believe he'd thoroughly explored every possible facet of this mysterious can was to go through with a taste test. Hey, if pot brownies were a thing, why not infuse soda with something? It was possible, right?

He had no idea. But he knew he was going to have to try. He looked at himself in the mirror above the sink and held up the can in a toast. "Well, Lance, here's to you. Good luck."

He took the tiniest sip he could manage.

Tasted nothing but syrup and artificial sweetener.

It was disgusting. Yet it tasted exactly like he expected it should.

He made a frustrated noise from deep down in his throat and then, after only the slightest hesitation, tipped the can to his lips and chugged a third of it.

How long do I give it? he wondered. *Five minutes? Ten?*

In the end, he waited fifteen minutes, sitting on the floor

with his back against the glass wall of the shower stall, waiting for his body or mind to react. Waited for the room to start spinning or to start hallucinating aliens taking a poop on the toilet. Waiting for anything that might signal there was something foreign in his system.

After fifteen minutes, he felt exactly the same, except for the tingling in his legs from where they'd started to fall asleep. He stood up and dumped the rest of the soda down the drain, turning on the hot water tap and rinsing away the remnants. Then he rinsed the inside of the can as well before feeling ridiculous as he closed one eye and then squinted, trying to look inside, as if there might be a message inscribed on the interior walls. Of course, he could see nothing, especially without some sort of flashlight.

I need to cut it open.

He left the bathroom and returned to his room, tossing the empty and well-rinsed can onto the bed and then unzipping the small side pouch of his backpack, where he kept his pocket knife. He pulled it free from the Velcro strap that kept it in place and then opened the blade. He reached for the can and—

Noticed the tiny words stamped on the underside of the can, where one usually found the packaging and expiration date. It looked ... wrong.

Lance scooped up the can and read the words, red and faint and stamped on almost haphazardly.

It was not a packaging or expiration date.

The top line of text was a website address that looked odd, but it was certainly not the website for the soda manufacturer. The bottom line was a series of twelve characters comprised of random letters and numbers.

Lance did not own a computer, and not even—again, much to his increasing chagrin—a smartphone with a built-in web browser. He could try and find a library, or maybe see if Loraine

Linklatter had a computer with Internet he could use, but he had a feeling that whatever this strange-looking web address led to might not be something he wanted random persons to see him browsing. No, this needed to be done in private, just in case.

Lance sat on the bed for a long time, staring at the bottom of the soda can in his hand and thinking about whether or not he should do what he was thinking.

On one hand, it seemed to go against what he'd been believing to be the best way to handle things. *For her protection*, he'd said, knowing there was a lot of truth to that statement. But on the other hand, when he really thought about the logistics of what he was asking here, he didn't see how it would actually cause her any physical danger, nor connect her directly to him.

In the end, he decided he would ask her. And he would hate himself forever if it turned out he was wrong.

He found his cell phone and typed out the message, hitting Send and feeling an odd sense of liberation, as if he were suddenly breaking free of a snare that had been holding him back. But along with that feeling came a sudden sense of anticipation that bordered on nervousness. When his phone chirped a couple minutes later, he actually felt his heartrate kick up as he punched the buttons to bring up the new message he'd received. He read it.

Leah: *Sure! But I'm pulling a double and can't till after my shift tonight. That cool?*

Lance smiled. *Yeah*, he thought. *That's completely cool.*

He sent his response and then closed his phone, tossing it on the bed next to him and leaning his head back, letting his eyes close. He was all at once very comfortable, very relaxed. Even though he knew it couldn't be possible, he could swear he could hear the waves crashing on the surf.

The nap began to envelop him, and he didn't fight it.

HER
(II)

Annabelle's Apron was busier than usual for a Saturday night in Westhaven, where Friday nights were usually the big tip nights, as it seemed like half the town piled in to scarf down some burgers or steaks or a full stack of pancakes for dinner before rushing back out the door and over to the high school to watch the football game (or basketball, once the seasons switched), leaving the waitresses and kitchen staff buried beneath mountains of dirty dishes and an all-at-once-silent dining room.

Once the game started, nobody came in. That was an exaggeration, of course. They did get the handful of regular customers who understood the routine and waited on purpose for the game to start before venturing out for a quiet dinner, the sounds of air horns blaring and the siren from the ambulance *whoop-whooping* after every Westhaven touchdown still audible, even way out at the diner. But this meager crowd of non-sports enthusiasts was nothing compared to the army that had preceded it.

Or maybe Annabelle's Apron wasn't that busy for a Saturday night, not really. Maybe it just seemed that way to Leah, because for the first time in several weeks, she had something she was desperately looking forward to once her shift ended and she'd wiped down her last table and rolled her last bundle of silverware. Something other than a hot shower and an evening binge-watching Netflix.

The text message from Lance had come in right as the lunch rush was winding down—no *Ghostbusters* alert tone in the diner, though. Margie was very strict about personal cell phone noises in the dining room, said it was unprofessional. Leah had felt the vibration from her phone in her back pocket and snuck a glance at it while she waited for a fresh pot of coffee to finish brewing.

She smiled. Couldn't help it.

After her night of tossing and turning in her bed, getting little sleep, all because she felt like she'd crossed a line, broken one of their unspoken relationship rules and potentially ruined what little momentum they'd been gaining, she'd been happy to get his message in the morning. It was simple and casual and to the point—*Just like him*, she'd thought, feeling that warmth in her chest—but she also couldn't help but feel it was forced. Like maybe he was still slightly peeved or put off by her questions, but wanted to play nice about it so as to not make her feel bad.

God, Leah, you're being such a girl, she'd chastised herself as she got ready for work. *Stop reading so much into this.*

But she couldn't help it. Lance was special, she could feel that in every bone of her body, and more importantly, he'd seemed to think she was special, too, and treated her like he did. Which, Leah reasoned with herself, was probably the most special thing of all. There was something between them. And she didn't ever want to let that go.

Which was why the message she'd gotten at the diner had made her so happy. It was as if the conversation of the previous night and this morning's had been wiped clean, and they were starting fresh.

Lance: *Hey there, I have a favor to ask you, whenever you have time to talk. Probably better to call instead of text.*

Not the most romantic of messages, she knew that, but it was a message all the same. He wanted to talk to her.

She'd responded, telling him it would have to wait till after the dinner shift. There was part of her that badly wanted to call him on her thirty-minute break in between lunch and dinner shifts, but that was when she ate and chatted with the other waitresses, and while honestly none of those things mattered so much that she would mind skipping them, she didn't want to have to constrain whatever conversation she and Lance needed to have to a defined window of time.

And something else told her she would probably want some privacy. She doubted very much that Lance would be calling her to ask something he wanted everyone to know about. Otherwise, he could have very easily asked somebody else, wherever he was.

So, she kept herself busy. Rolled her silverware and helped clean the countertops and started reorganizing the shelves of condiments with such focus that Margie stopped by and stared for a moment, as if trying to come up with some sort of witty retort about Leah's sudden burst of *Look what a good employee I am*, but in the end she just nodded, satisfied, and went to refill Hank Peterson's coffee.

Finally, her last table left. Leah cleared away the dirty dishes, wiped the table down, bade farewell to Margie and Hank and the other two waitresses who were working the closing shift, and then nearly sprinted out the door with one arm in her jacket and the other one out.

The walk back to her studio apartment, which she normally enjoyed—especially in the crisp evenings when the temperatures began to drop—seemed to take a very long time.

She forced herself to take a shower, wanting to cleanse herself of the lingering smell of grease and coffee and bleach, and then, once she'd dried herself and dressed in sweats and a t-shirt, switching on the little space heater next to her bed, she leaned back against her pillows, stretched her legs out, getting comfortable, and called him.

Put the phone to her ear and listened as it rang, hearing the blood pumping through her head as her heart kicked up a beat or two. It suddenly felt very strange, to actually be calling him, about to *speak* to him after all this time. She was oddly nervous, even though she knew she had no reason to be. It was just Lance. After what they'd been through, after what he'd done for Leah and her father—and the entire town, really—she would have thought nerves were something she wouldn't have to worry about.

She heard the connection pick up on the other end. Then, his voice: "Thank goodness you called."

Her heart dropped. Worry set in. "Why? What's wrong?"

She heard what sounded like him yawning. "I was taking maybe the best nap ever, and if you hadn't called, I might have slept right through dinner."

Her brain, slow on the uptake, not expecting the humor after being so frozen with dread, finally allowed her to laugh. "You're an idiot."

"I'm serious," he said, though she heard the playfulness in his voice. "When my blood sugar gets low ... watch out. I'm useless and grumpy and generally unpleasant. So I've been told."

"You're an idiot," she said again, wondering if he can hear the smile beaming on her face.

"You know," he said, "I've imagined what we might say to each other, once we finally got to talk again, and I have to say, I wasn't predicting so many insults."

"So you've been fantasizing about me, is that what you're saying?" Leah sat up on the bed, loving how easily they were falling back in stride, wondering why on earth she'd been nervous.

Silence from his end.

She took advantage. "I mean, I wouldn't blame you if you have been. I'm pretty amazing, you know."

There was another beat of silence, but then he offered: "Yes. Yes, you are." And the sincerity she heard through the speaker filled her with adoration.

"I've missed you," he said. "Missed talking to you."

"Me too," she said. And they enjoyed this moment between them, the space between pleasantries and what they both knew was the real reason for the call. The favor he'd alluded to earlier.

"So what is it you want me to do?" she asked, taking the lead.

He was quiet for several seconds, and Leah wondered if he was now second-guessing his idea, had decided that maybe reaching out to her wasn't the right thing to do. But then he started talking. He told her everything—not where he was, but about the girls with the coolers and the feeling he was getting and about the soda can and the web address with the code he'd found.

And then he told her about the suicides, how it seemed to be a pandemic, and to make things worse, there might be somebody helping things along.

"I don't think they're related," he told her. "The girls and the suicides, I mean. But..." He paused. "I think I'm here for both. I think I'm supposed to help with all of it."

Leah absorbed it all, marveled at the potential scope of it. "How?" she asked incredulously.

He actually laughed out loud at this. "I never know," he says. "Until I do."

Leah heard this answer and had a difficult time comprehending the selflessness of this man's life, his daily actions. She'd only met him as he'd saved her town from a great Evil, but she knew he'd done so much before her, and there was no telling how much more good he'd spread, how many more people he'd save after.

She shook her head. "What great things you do, Lance." She

meant these words with every bit of her being but fully expected some sort of witty or sarcastic remark from him, a downplaying of his own abilities. But instead … just silence. Long and drawn out and so jarring that Leah pulled the phone away from her face to check the screen and make sure the call hadn't gotten disconnected.

"Lance?" she asked. "Are you still there?"

She heard him swallow, an audible click in his throat, and then take a deep breath. "Yes," he said. "I'm here. Sorry, it's just…" He trailed off, and silence replaced the words again.

"What is it?"

A pause. Then, "My mother. She said almost the exact same thing to me the night she died."

"Oh, Lance, I'm so sorry. I had no idea. I just …"

"It's okay," he told her. "Really. It's actually … well, it's okay, trust me. It just sorta, you know, caught me off guard."

She said nothing. What could she say?

There was silence again, a moment of refocusing, before Leah decided to push forward. Asked, "So what can I do to help?"

He told her, stressing over and over again that she didn't have to. That he'd completely understand if she didn't want to get involved in any way. She dismissed his caution for her and joked that if he'd at least gone and gotten himself a smartphone, he could have taken care of this himself.

"Yeah, I know," he said. "I'll put one on my Christmas list, alright?"

And suddenly Leah was overwhelmed by one of the saddest images she'd ever conjured. She pictured Lance alone, sitting in some run-down motel—much like the one she'd met him in, the one she used to run with her father—with nobody to share the holidays with. No family. No friends.

"I'll do it," she blurted, trying to push back the tears that had surprised her. "I'll check it out and let you know what I find."

"Thank you," he said, giving her the web address and the code he'd found. She put him on speakerphone and typed these into the Notes app on her phone.

"Got it," she said.

"Okay, I'll talk to you soon. And, Leah?"

"Yes?"

"Be careful?"

She said she would, and then they hung up.

[19]

Lance ended the call and flipped his phone shut, bathing himself in darkness. The little sliver of screen on the top of his phone displayed the time, and he saw it was half past eight. He sat up in the bed, reaching out for the bedside light and switching it on. Rubbed his eyes and swung his legs over the edge, marveling at how long he'd slept.

When was the last time you napped like that?

He didn't know. A long time, for sure. But the bed was comfortable, and the setting peaceful. Despite his being needed here—for by now, he knew it was no accident he'd ended up in Sugar Beach—he had to wonder if the Universe was allowing him to rest, as well. And because of that, he wondered if this much-needed sleep was a reward for hard work done thus far, or preparation for a tough battle ahead. He chose not to debate the issue.

It'd felt so good to hear her voice. A swirl of emotions had stirred, taking him by surprise as he'd been jarred awake by his phone's robotic ringtone and had seen her name flash across the tiny screen. He'd answered, and after all these weeks ... it'd been like no time had passed at all.

135

How he'd missed her.

But now, even though he'd felt confident in asking, had assured himself there would be no harm in the matter, he felt guilty for getting her involved, even in such a seemingly anonymous way.

His stomach grumbled, and he pushed the negative thoughts away. Pulled on his sneakers and went out into the hallway, stopping at the restroom before heading down the stairs to the foyer.

The house was quiet and still. He stood there, by the front door, hearing nothing but the ticking of the clock and the hum of electricity burning in the lights.

"Hello?" he called out.

Nothing.

He shrugged, walked to the kitchen and found a note written on the digital screen of the high-tech refrigerator. The handwriting was flowy, with lots of loops. A woman's writing.

Lance, went out for a bit. Make yourself at home. – L

Loraine Linklatter was a very trusting person, it seemed. Leaving him, a stranger, all alone in her large home. But, Lance supposed, that was the sort of risk you took on when you decided to operate a B&B. He reached for the fridge's door handle, ready to retrieve his sub sandwich from earlier, and just as he was about to pull the door open, something on the digital screen caught his eye. There, along the left side of the screen in the Notes application where Loraine had scrawled her message, was a list of other saved notes, one of which was labeled TAKE-OUT AND DELIVERY FOOD.

Lance selected the note, Loraine's written message disappearing and a new note opening. A short typed-out list of restaurants and phone numbers was displayed, obviously meant to help guests who were in search of food. Lance, who'd been ready to unapologetically devour his sub, found his eyes instantly landing on one item on the list. *Frank's Pizza*. And before he even knew what he was doing, his cell phone was in hand and he'd ordered a large pie loaded with meats and veggies. Not knowing his actual address, he'd simply said he was staying at the Boundary House, and the man on the phone said his food would be there in twenty minutes.

Lance hung up, all thoughts of his sub forgotten, and headed out onto the porch, thinking he'd enjoy the evening air in one of the porch swings while he waited for his food.

After all, how often was he at the beach?

───

While he waited, alone with his thoughts and the one-sided conversation with the ceramic frog on the porch, Lance saw the warm orange glow flickering on the horizon above the dunes across the street.

They're back, he thought and wondered how long they'd been coming to that spot and how long they'd stay.

The pizza arrived right on time, Lance paying cash and tipping the driver and bidding him a good night. Once the delivery car had driven away, back up Sand Dollar Road, Lance turned and looked at the frog, who seemed to be eyeing the pizza box in Lance's hands with intense focus.

"Look, I'd offer you a slice," Lance said, "But don't you mostly eat bugs?"

The frog did not answer, and Lance took this as silent resignation.

He took his pizza and went down the porch steps, working

his way through the gate and across the road, through the empty park and over the dunes.

And they were there, the five of them. The college kids from the night before. Three were seated on the pieces of driftwood—two boys together on one side, one of the girls alone on the opposite. Down by the water, the other girl—the one with the long hair who Lance had assumed was older than the others—and boy stood side by side just on the edge of the surf as it rolled in and out.

The bonfire burned bright in the center of it all. Flames leaping and wood cracking, flooding a wide circle of light out around them all, and Lance wondered which of them had started it.

The girl who sat alone on the one piece of driftwood looked away from the flames and saw Lance standing there at the end of the path. She didn't look particularly friendly or unfriendly, but there was recognition there, and Lance raised one hand in a wave. She waved back, and he made his way through the sand and over to her. "Hi, I'm Lance," he said. "May I join you all?"

The girl nodded, red hair splayed around a freckled face which she brushed out of her eyes. She was wearing cutoff denim shorts and a tank top, freckles peppering her shoulders in the golden light from the fire. Lance sat next to her on the driftwood, taking a moment to find a comfortable position, his enormous sneakers troublesome in the sand. He left a good amount of space between he and her, setting the pizza box in the open space dividing them and opening it, selecting a slice and taking a bite. He chewed, staring into the flames, and after he'd swallowed, he said, "I saw you guys last night, if you remember. Thought maybe I'd come back and see if you all were here again. I don't get to hang out with people my own age very often."

He took another bite and waited to see if she'd answer.

She turned to face him, pulling one leg up under her. "We're here every night. There doesn't seem to be anywhere else to go."

Lance nodded. "Yeah, the Sand Crab doesn't seem like my sort of joint either. Never been big on alcohol, or the bar scene ... or country music, really."

She laughed, and it was the first semblance of emotion Lance had seen from her. "Let me guess," she said, "you played basketball—because you just look the type—and you're a hip-hop fan."

Lance popped the last bit of his pizza slice into his mouth and swallowed. Picked up another slice, smiling and nodding. "Good guess," he said. "Yes, I did play basketball, but no, not a hip-hop fan. I'm not really a big music fan in general, to be honest. My mother, though, she always was..."

He trailed off, catching himself. Fought back the image of Pamela Brody swaying to the live music that night, dancing like nobody was watching in the Hillston Farmer's Market's parking lot while the live band rocked the crowd. It was only a very short time before she'd died.

"She's dead," the girl said knowingly.

He nodded.

"I'm sorry," she said.

"Thank you." He ate in silence for a while, watching the flames and hearing the waves crash to his left.

One of the boys from the other piece of driftwood across the fire spoke for the first time, asking, "Why are you here?"

He was pale and short, wearing blue jeans and a baggy hoodie. He had the hood pulled over his head and his hands tucked into the front pocket of the sweatshirt.

Lance felt the weight of the question.

"I'm here to help people," he said, much like he'd told Todd from the diner.

"Who?" the boy asked, sitting forward.

"You know," Lance said, "I haven't quite figured it all out yet."

The boy nodded, as if this made complete sense. The boy next to him, taller and more muscular, wearing board shorts and a t-shirt and a baseball cap on backwards, asked, "Do you know how long you'll stay?"

"No," Lance said. "I usually don't." He finished his next slice of pizza, and his curiosity won him over. "What about you all?" he asked. "What brought you here?"

The girl and boy that had been down by the surf were now standing off to the side, in between the two pieces of driftwood, having made their way up from the water. Up close, Lance verified his assumption of the girl being a bit older than the rest, and the boy as well. Not much, only a couple years, but still, there was more wisdom, a different presence in their eyes.

"Hard to say," the woman said. "We all just felt drawn here." As she said the words, she nodded toward the fire, the scene before her. "Does that make any sense to you?"

Lance remembered his walk on the beach the night before, how he'd been so tired but had all at once felt compelled to make his way toward these flames, this group. *There's an answer here*, he thought to himself before saying, "Yes. That makes complete sense."

The woman's body relaxed, her shoulders loosening, as if Lance's understanding was some great relief. Then she said, "We just keep coming back." And then she turned and made her way back down to the water.

Eventually, the other two boys got up from their seats and made their way down the sand, standing side by side with the others by the water, leaving Lance and the girl with the red hair alone. Nobody here seemed particularly fond of conversation, and Lance figured this was one of the reasons they had all managed to find themselves together. Finishing all the pizza he wanted and closing the box, he looked at the girl and asked, "Okay, you pegged me as the basketball player, and I'll give you that one, even though it was easy. But what else is it you see when you look at me?"

The girl tucked her hair behind her ear again and didn't even look at him. Simply said, "I see a boy who's trying really hard."

Lance was about to chime in, make a quip about how ambiguous a statement that was, even though he was startled at its accuracy. But the girl quickly turned and looked him in the eye. "But," she said, "he needs to realize he doesn't always have to do it alone."

Then, without another word, she stood and went to join her group by the surf.

Lance sat quietly for a long time, one burning question blazing hot as the bonfire across his mind.

Who are you all?

[20]

LANCE FOUND THE GARBAGE BIN ALONG THE FENCE NEAR the gate of the Boundary House and tossed his pizza box into it, one remaining piece left inside—a treat for a lucky rat or stray cat who might be patrolling the dump. Lance wasn't usually one to waste food, but he found he didn't have the patience to lug the box and extra slice into the Boundary House's fancy kitchen and search for aluminum foil or a plastic baggy in which to store it until he was ready to eat again. He found he couldn't focus on much of anything except the parting words the redheaded girl by the bonfire had offered him before she had gone off to join the rest of her group by the water.

"He needs to realize he doesn't always have to do it alone."

There was a part of Lance that digested these words with a bit of hopefulness, thinking that the Universe was pointing him to Leah. But the practical side of him, the side of him that'd seen the Evil in this world, had narrowly escaped the Reverend and the Surfer and whatever plans they had for him, refused to believe it would ever be okay for him to bring her into his life any deeper than she was right now.

Not yet, anyway. It was way too soon.

But still ... the girl by the fire knew something about him. Though he knew very little about her.

Lance walked up the steps and across the porch, pushing through the door to the Boundary House and hearing noise from the kitchen. Loraine was back, and Lance was glad. He needed to pay her.

He ran up the stairs to his backpack and grabbed some cash, returning to the downstairs and finding Loraine Linklatter at the breakfast nook, sipping tea and reading a paperback novel. She looked up when he walked in and nodded at him with a weak smile.

"Hi," she said.

"Hi," Lance said, crossing the wood floor and asking, "Good night?"

Loraine shrugged. "About as good as it gets around here for me."

Lance didn't know what to say to that. The woman's energy, which had seemed plentiful upon his arrival, and her mood, which had seemed abundantly pleasant, had both dropped off a cliff.

Instead, he asked, "How much is it for the two nights? I'd like to pay you now. You know"—he shrugged—"so you know I'm not a freeloader."

Lance gave a small grin of his own, seeing if Loraine would rise to the challenge of returning it, but instead all she did was give him a dollar amount which he found incredibly low, considering the accommodations. Lance peeled off some bills from his stack of cash—he'd need to find an ATM soon—and laid the amount on the table.

"Thank you," Loraine said.

"No, thank *you*. This place is very nice. You could probably charge a lot more than that and still be packed during the summer months, right?"

"Lance, I want to apologize to you." Her words came out fast and short, as if she'd been winding up to pitch them out and finally decided now was the time.

"I'm sorry?" Lance said, confused.

"For earlier," Loraine said. "I was prying into your life, and I was clearly making you uncomfortable, and I should have stopped. So..." She sighed and took a sip of her tea. "I just want you to know I'm sorry. For that, and then the way I shut down when you asked about whether I was married. It's just ... I was..."

Tears welled up in Loraine Linklatter's eyes, and Lance slid into the breakfast nook opposite her, wanting to make himself appear less opposing to this woman in her vulnerable state. Something was happening here, a moment that Lance felt was important.

Loraine gave off a weak laugh and wiped her eyes. Took a long sip of her tea and swallowed loudly. "It's still hard, even after all this time. After Daisy, well... her father took her death very badly—and I don't blame him, not at all. I mean, who really knows how to prepare themselves for the death of their child?"

Or their own parents, Lance thought. Though he knew there was a difference. One he couldn't begin to understand.

"But he ..." Loraine continued. "Instead of getting help, or letting us try to work through it together, he left me." She snapped her fingers. "Just like that. Here one minute, gone the next, like a fucking magic trick." She caught herself. "Sorry for the language."

Lance shrugged. "S'okay." People shouldn't be expected to censor themselves while emotional.

Loraine stood from the table and walked her cup of tea to the sink, dumping out the rest and rinsing it out. "Anyway," she said, recomposing herself, "he left me, so within a month, I'd lost my baby girl and my husband. I don't know where he is, and honestly I haven't tried looking that hard." She shrugged. "He could be dead, for all I know."

She took a deep breath and grabbed a dish towel to begin drying the teacup. "So when you asked me about him earlier ... well, how could you have possibly known? So, I'm sorry. I guess I didn't expect the wound to still be so fresh. I apologize if I was rude. I hope you can forgive me."

But I did know, Lance thought. *Not all of it, but I knew it would sting.*

Lance and Loraine Linklatter bade each other goodnight, and Lance headed up the stairs, not sure what he was going to do since he'd only been up a few hours since his marathon nap. His head was swimming with contradicting emotions: confusion and frustration, sympathy and compassion. He felt bad for Loraine Linklatter and all she'd been through, worse still that he'd set her up earlier with his question about her husband, but all the same, there was a tugging coming from elsewhere that was trying to pull him toward another side of the story, another angle he was not seeing.

Because—

He opened the door to his bedroom and found Daisy sitting in the same chair where he'd found her waiting last night. At the sight of him, her face lit up in a smile that melted him.

"Can you read to me?" she asked cheerfully.

Because why is she here?

"DYING TO FIGURE OUT WHAT HAPPENS NEXT, HUH?" Lance asked, walking across the room and sitting on the edge of the bed to face Daisy in the chair. Then, embarrassed, he realized what a poor expression that had been (*dying* to figure out what happens next) and quickly continued, "Yeah, Coben's good at that, isn't he?"

Daisy didn't seem too concerned with the novel's mystery, however. She just jumped from the chair, climbed over Lance and assumed the same position she'd been in the night before as he'd read to her—lying back on the covers with her head against the pillow, hands crossed in that same way that brought to mind corpses. Lance swiveled around to face her, kicking his sneakers off and pulling his legs up onto the bed.

"Daisy, I'll read to you, I promise, but can I ask you a few things first?"

Daisy, who'd had her eyes closed in mock sleep, opened them and looked at Lance with excitement. "Is it like a game? A guessing game?"

Lance pursed his lips. "Um, no, not really."

Daisy's face fell. "So, it's like questions on a test?" she asked with complete contempt.

Lance shook his head, trying to quickly think of an approach that might spark some interest in Daisy long enough for her to help him, or at least for him to get a couple answers that might lead to something else that could help him.

"Daisy, you're a big girl, and very smart, right?"

The compliment struck gold, and Daisy's face perked up. She nodded. "Yes, I am. Mommy always told me so."

"Well, I'm sure she's right," Lance said. "So, the thing is, I need some help, and I think you're one of the only people who can actually help me. Because you're so smart, I think that together we can figure something out. So, what do you say? Can I ask you a few things and see what you think? I think you have the answer I'm looking for."

"Is it because I'm dead?" Daisy asked. "Is that why you think I'm the one that can help you?"

Lance smiled, a genuine show of admiration. "You *are* a very smart girl, Daisy. I wouldn't lie to you. So, yes. That's part of the reason I think you can help me."

Daisy sat up a bit, thankfully unfolding her hands from in front of her and leaning back on her elbows. "Thought so," she said. Then, as if she suddenly possessed all the power in the conversation, she asked, "What do you want to know?"

Lance stood from the bed, walked in front of it and started pacing back and forth. When Daisy looked at him with raised eyebrows, he said, "Sorry, helps me think." Then, after a few seconds, he started with what he figured to be the simplest question. "Daisy, why do you think you're here?"

The question, which had seemed simple when it had left Lance's mind, suddenly loomed very large in the room, and he realized its enormity. He could see the same sense of realization on Daisy's face, so he walked her through it.

"What I mean is," Lance said, "when you passed away, why did you stay here and not go off to be where ... wherever else the rest of the people who've passed on go to?"

Daisy answered immediately. "Oh, that's easy. I didn't want to leave Mommy."

Lance, while moved by the girl's love for her mother—an emotion he could very much relate to—figured this to be an incorrect answer. Maybe not in Daisy's mind, but certainly in the Universe's grand scheme. Lance didn't believe, in his experience, that spirits had the ability to choose when they moved on —not completely, that is. More often than not, they were left here because of an unfinished task, incomplete business, or— especially in the cases of the beings that Lance had encountered —they were waiting for someone to show up.

Him.

Though Lance didn't think that the spirits actually knew that they were waiting for him. To them, they must think...

Okay, Lance didn't know what they must think as they lingered in between worlds.

The longer he lived, the more he realized how little he knew about any of this. His gifts and abilities showed him much more than other people were ever cursed to know, but for every question he had answered, a hundred more arrived in its place.

"I understand," Lance said. "You must love your mommy very much, right?"

Daisy smiled and nodded. "She's the best mommy in the whole world!"

"I bet," Lance said. "And I know she loves you very much."

Daisy beamed. "Oh yeah, she does!" And then, "Do you have a mommy?"

And where ordinarily Lance would have expected himself to feel sad, to briefly succumb to that icy bath of loneliness that often accompanied thoughts of his mother, instead he found himself suddenly remembering several of the happiest times they'd spent together. Birthdays and holidays and days at the library and evenings in their kitchen sharing a pie.

"I did," Lance said. "She died."

Daisy grew somber for a moment, but then her eyes grew wide and she said, "But wait, you can still see her! If you can see me, that must mean you can see her too, right?"

And here came the sadness. Lance smiled and shook his head. "No, Daisy. I can't see her. I don't get to pick who I see and who I don't."

"Oh," Daisy said. "Well, that sucks."

Lance laughed, loud and deep. "Yes, Daisy, that does suck. We can agree on that. Now, can you think of any other reason why maybe you stayed here after you passed away? Other than the fact you wanted to stay with your mommy?"

"Can you read to me now?" Daisy said, looking away.

It was the first time she'd taken her eyes off him, Lance realized.

"Daisy," Lance said, trying not to sound too much like a parent reprimanding their child. "Do you know another reason why you're still here?"

Daisy shook her head, still not making eye contact with him. "We don't have to read that book again if you don't want," she said. "We can do one of the other ones. I don't care."

Lance walked around to Daisy's side of the bed and sat on the edge, sitting silently for a long time until eventually the girl turned her head to look and see what he was doing, and that's when Lance saw something that looked like embarrassment in her eyes, her cheeks.

"Daisy?"

"I don't know where to go!" the little girl cried. "I can't leave! I know I'm not supposed to be here. I'm supposed to go to the other place, but I'm stuck! I can't find my way! Can you help me? Can you help unstuck me? I don't know where to go!"

The words rushed from her mouth, and without thinking, Lance reached out, ready to envelop the child in his arms and hug her tight and stroke her hair and whisper to her that everything was going to be alright.

But, of course, his hands and arms passed right through Daisy's image, grabbing nothing but the pillows and comforter. She looked at him, such sadness in her eyes, and in that moment Lance would have done anything to make her happy again. Daisy thought she was stuck, that she didn't know the way, but in reality, Lance figured the Universe was simply keeping her here for him. And for that, Lance felt incredibly guilty.

"Hey," he said, "how about I read to you now?"

Daisy's face was awash with relief, and she smiled big and settled herself back into her listening position. Lance walked around the bed and lay down next to her, reaching for the novel on the nightstand and finding his place. He started to read.

Thirty minutes later, after Daisy's spirit had vanished from the bed and Lance found himself enthralled in the mystery on the pages, there was the sound of footsteps in the hallway, and then the stairs. Muffled conversation from the floor below. A moment later, there was a loud knock on Lance's bedroom door.

"Come in," Lance said.

Loraine Linklatter cracked the door open and stuck her head in. "There's a girl downstairs looking for you."

[22]

LANCE'S HEAD DID A QUICK DIZZY DANCE OF CONFUSION, repeating Loraine Linklatter's words in his mind—*There's a girl downstairs looking for you*—and for the tiniest of moments, just a fleeting surge of excitement and happiness, he allowed himself to imagine Leah standing downstairs in the foyer, waiting for him to come down the stairs toward her like an inverse prom night pickup.

But that was ridiculous. He knew it was impossible. He'd spoken to Leah just a couple hours ago, and there was no way she'd have been able to somehow do detective work and track him down and then get all the way from Westhaven to Sugar Beach in that time. No matter how badly part of Lance wished she had.

"A girl?" Lance asked, sitting up on the bed. He cast a quick glance to his right, just to be sure, wondering if Daisy would return at the sight of her mother. But no, Daisy had apparently only come for her bedtime story.

Loraine Linklatter pushed the door open further, and Lance saw she was wearing the same thin robe she'd been wearing last night when he'd arrived. "Yes. And in the future, I'd appreciate it if you could let me know when you'll be having guests."

"I..." Lance started, then cut himself off. He was about to say that he hadn't been expecting anybody, but he thought the notion of letting Loraine Linklatter know there was a stranger downstairs waiting in her house might not be the best idea—especially if they weren't a paying customer. "I'm sorry," was what he did say. "Slipped my mind."

Loraine nodded, apparently accepting the apology, then said, "I'm going back to bed. You know your way around the kitchen, if she'd like anything to eat or drink. I only ask that you please try and clean up after yourselves." Then she smiled, gave Lance a wink and thumbs-up, and said, "Good job, Lance. She's a cutie."

"Uh ... yes, ma'am. Thank you, ma'am."

What else was he supposed to say?

Loraine left the door open but retreated into the hallway, the sound of her footfalls fading away toward her bedroom. Once Lance heard her bedroom door open and close, he stood, pulled on his sneakers, and then walked out into the hall.

He'd made it two steps toward the stairs when his cell phone buzzed in his pocket, a quick one-two-three vibration. He pulled the phone out and glanced at the screen.

Leah.

He sighed, hating himself for ignoring the call and shoving the phone back in his pocket. Wished he could telepathically send her a note letting her know he was in the middle of something. Even a message that short would take too long to peck out on his old-school phone. His curiosity about who was waiting for him was too strong, too much the priority.

Lance was halfway down the stairs when he saw her. Blond hair, pretty face, same sweatpants and sweatshirt as earlier.

The girl who'd been selling sodas by the donut shop.

Diana. Eyes darting around the foyer like a scared animal.

"Hi," Lance said, stepping down from the last stair.

And at the sight of him, Diana's face softened, her shoulders relaxed, and she looked at him with pleading eyes. "You help me?"

What else could he say?

"Yes."

And Diana closed the distance between them in a rush of movement and threw her arms around him, hugging him tight and burying her face into his chest as she cried.

Lance, surprised by the sudden reaction, gently returned the hug, reaching up and stroking the girl's head and whispering that everything was going to be alright.

Just like he'd wanted to do for Daisy.

He hoped he wasn't making promises he couldn't keep.

Lance got Diana settled in the kitchen, seating her in the breakfast nook while he made her some tea. After delivering the beverage, he asked, "Are you hungry?"

Diana nodded, taking the tea in her hands and clutching the mug as if it were a life preserver. Lance opened the fridge, saw his sub he'd never eaten and pulled it out, unwrapping it and setting it on the table. "Hope you like turkey," he said.

Diana picked up one half of the sandwich and began to eat, and when she picked up the mug of tea again, Lance noticed that her hands were shaking, the liquid splashing over the edge of the cup. He stood and got some paper towels. Brought them back to the table and slid into the opposite side of the breakfast nook.

She's afraid, he thought. But of what?

The two of them sat there, quietly. Lance watched her finish off half the sub and then the tea, never taking his eyes off her. She would look up at him occasionally but then quickly cast her eyes back down to her food. She seemed timid, unsure of what she was really doing.

When she took it upon herself to rewrap the last half of the sub and push it back toward Lance, he asked, "Feel better?"

Diana said nothing.

Lance nodded. "I know I always feel better after eating. Can I get you anything else?"

When Diana didn't answer—not really, anyway, just a small shake of the head—Lance figured he'd have to be direct if he was going to get anywhere with this girl. She'd made it this far—finding him where he'd told her he'd be—but now it was as if she'd hit a wall and didn't know how to keep moving forward with whatever plan she might have convinced herself she had.

Lance thought about the black Ford Excursion, dropping off and picking up the girls, remembered the security cameras on the house he'd gone to spy on with Todd earlier. Considered the girl's fear. He asked, "Did you run away? Sneak out of the house?"

Diana looked up to him and for the first time held his gaze, pretty blue eyes locking onto his. Her hair fell softly around her features, spilling past her shoulders.

"Yes," she said. A short and clipped syllable, her accent strong.

Lance thought about the girl's shaking hands as she'd sipped the tea.

"And are you afraid they're going to find you and take you back?"

"Yes." No hesitation. No thinking. Just fact. "They will be mad. Make me pay more."

"Pay more?" Lance asked, leaning back and trying not to make the conversation seem like an interrogation.

"Yes."

"Pay more ... money?"

Diana opened her mouth to speak, then stopped. Cocked her head to the side, thinking. "Yes. John's money. I work and John pay. If I go back, I must work more and—"

And the tears came then, Diana's face all at once flushing with pain and sadness and fear and she let out a soft gasp as she let go. She cried into her hands, shaking her head, her shoulders heaving. Lance sat, patient and quiet, waiting for the girl to recompose herself, feeling the sadness in his chest grow with each pain-filled wail she spilled into her cupped hands. Wondered just what sort of hell she'd been through.

After a couple minutes, Diana managed to calm herself and looked up, first wiping at her face with the sleeves of her sweatshirt and then reaching for a paper towel. Lance handed her one and she said, "Thank you," Taking it and wiping her nose and cheeks. When she'd finished cleaning herself up, she looked at Lance and said. "Please, take me away. I no want to go back to house. I no want to go *home*. They might make me. Go home—worse than working more."

Lance, more confused at the girl's words than ever, nodded his head. "Okay. Don't worry. I'm not taking you back. I'll help you, I promise."

He said this and wondered what he was going to do, where he was going to take this girl. He didn't know exactly what was going on, but judging by the fear in Diana's eyes, he had no doubt that once whoever owned the house with the security cameras realized she was missing, they'd come looking for her. And something told Lance they weren't going to ask him very nicely to hand her over if they were to find the two of them together.

I need more information, he thought. *She's got to tell me more.*

"Diana," he started. "Who's John? What work are you doing for him?"

Diana looked at Lance, and something like confusion washed over her face, as if his question didn't quite make sense. Then she said, "A lot of names."

Now it was Lance's turn to be confused. "A lot of names? John has lots of names? Like, people call him names other than John?"

Diana made a face again, and as she was about to speak, Lance's cell phone buzzed in his pocket again. He pulled it free and saw Leah's name on the screen. She was calling back, pressing him to answer.

She must have found what I asked for, Lance thought. Then, needing a small break from the confusion that was growing with his conversation with Diana, Lance said, "I have to take this." Then added, "It's a friend who can help."

He flipped the phone open and answered the call.

HER
(III)

It took Leah almost an hour after she'd ended the call with Lance before she finally clicked open a new web browser tab on her laptop (a private browsing window—*incognito*, the browser called it—something she'd always heard people joke about as the way men looked at porn without their girlfriends or wives finding them out if they happened to snoop on their men's web history) and typed in the address that Lance had given her. The delay was partly because she'd started watching *Stranger Things*, desperately wanting to see how things ended up for the kids in Hawkins, but also because she knew that there was the chance that once she did what Lance had asked her, even though on the surface it seemed very simple and with very few serious long-term repercussions, she would be crossing a line that she might not ever be able to go back from.

She'd be officially involved.

Lance had warned her so strongly about this as their initial time together had come to an end, how being associated with him could be potentially dangerous, but as Leah looked around her tiny studio apartment and thought about her shifts at Annabelle's Apron and again shook her head in disbelief at how little of the world—hell, the *country*—she'd seen, how little she'd actually *lived*, she found the decision suddenly very easy.

Her mother and brother were dead, and her relationship with her father, while it was better now than it had been in years—thanks to Lance—was no longer enough to make her feel obligated into living the life she'd been dealt.

I've got nothing to lose, she thought and pressed the Enter key on the keyboard.

The page loaded. A solid black screen with a white box

labeled ACCESS CODE. She entered the code Lance had given her, her fingers hovering over the trackpad for just a split second—one final moment of deliberation—and then she clicked the arrow to enter the site.

She listened to the ringing in her ear as she called him. Cursed out loud when he didn't answer and threw the phone onto her bed, hanging up without leaving a message. This wasn't the sort of thing you tried to explain over a voicemail.

He's busy, she thought. *In the middle of something—and honestly, when is he not in the middle of something?*

She tried to relax, convince herself that Lance had not fallen prey to some harm in the time since they'd last spoken. On her laptop—which now felt tainted and in need of a full scan from her antivirus software—she switched back to her Netflix window and tried resuming *Stranger Things.*

But she couldn't focus. Had too many questions. She'd made it through just shy of half an episode—knowing she'd have to go back and watch it again because she couldn't recall a single thing that'd happened—before she picked up her phone and called Lance again, tapping the phone against her ear as it rang.

"Leah?" he answered.

"It's porn!" She didn't mean to yell and quickly covered her mouth with her free hand, a silly, instinctive gesture. Looked around the room as if there might have been somebody there to hear her. When she spoke again, she did it quietly. "Okay, maybe not, you know, a typical porn site. It's more of a webcam girl site," she said, "but ... there's more to it than just, well, you know, normal videos. It's very ... *boutique.*"

There was silence for a beat. Then, "Boutique?"

"Yes," she said.

"I'm ... I'm going to need you to elaborate."

She paused, thinking about everything she'd seen. "It's more intimate, like a personal, customizable experience."

"Customizable? Like when you order a Whopper from Burger King?"

"Are you always thinking about food?"

"Sorry. Go on."

She sighed and reeled in her thoughts. Organized them and then laid them out the best she could. "This site is niche," she said. "It's not just a bunch of videos of girls in their bedrooms taking off their clothes and getting off with sex toys while a thousand dudes jerk it in real time from the other end of the Internet."

"That's from Shakespeare, right? Which play?"

Leah ignored the joke and pressed on. "Now, of course, they *do* have that sort of thing, but that's the cheap stuff, some of it even free, like ... like an appetizer to get you excited about the main course."

"We're back to food again?"

"Now, once you get past the typical stuff, there's a whole other section of the site where customers can buy, and I quote, *Intimate companionship and experiences*. It's like ... it's like the girlfriend experience you'd get from an escort service, only ... this is just online."

"Girlfriend experience?" Lance asked. "What's that?"

"Seriously?"

"Pretend I know nothing about any of this. Because ... I don't, really."

"Is it weird I'm sort of impressed by that?"

Lance said, "Maybe. Just remember I didn't get out much growing up. I had ... other priorities."

Leah shook her head, so curious to learn more about Lance's childhood. She hoped she'd get the chance to have him tell her all about it one day. "The girlfriend experience is where a guy, or girl, I guess, hires a woman to act as his girlfriend, to pretend to be romantically involved. Not just to have sex. Now, don't kid yourself, the sex follows most of the time, I'm sure. But in this situation, the girl you pay for might, say, go out to dinner and a movie with you first. Talk about your friends and family and hobbies and, well … act like they actually give a damn about anything except getting freaky. It's all very sad, actually, if you ask me. People that are so desperate for love, they are willing to pay for it."

"So this site is offering a digital-only girlfriend experience. Is that what you're saying?"

"Yes, they allow you to actually pick a girl from a list of profiles and request them as your companion. After that, you get to have a one-time meet-and-greet chat—for free—and see if the two of you hit it off enough to proceed. If you do, you pay a boat-load of money—bitcoin only, of course—and the charade starts. It will last as long as you're willing to pay. Billed weekly."

"What's bitcoin?" Lance asked.

Leah sighed. "We don't have enough time for that."

"Okay."

"Anyway, if you don't really care about having a girl act like she's into you on a romantic level, you can also choose to just have the *customizable* experience. Which is basically—again, after paying a boatload of money—you can submit a form detailing exactly what sort of sexual fantasy or situation you'd like to have played out on-screen, and they'll do it. Anything you want, except for a very, *very* short list of banned suggestions. Basically anything short of killing somebody or causing extreme physical harm."

"How considerate of them," Lance said. Then he asked, "So why the soda cans and the special code? Seems like a pointless effort."

"I did some research on that. They don't actually mention any of that on the site itself, so I did some Googling. Turns out it's all part of the *boutique* process. By adding this extra level of effort, or, well, mystique to the process, they are essentially duping these customers into thinking this is an even more private and tailored experience. Like they're part of some secret club. I found a few message boards online dedicated to tracking down which cities have girls selling the codes, and where to find them. It's like a game. There's even speculation—which I don't believe—that certain cities have better codes that lead to hotter girls. It's crazy the amount of time people have spent on this. There's user-created maps online, showing which spots in the cities have been known to have girls selling codes, what time of day they're usually there, everything. Seriously, who has time for this sort of thing?"

Lance was quiet for a moment, then he said, "People who are lonely, I guess."

"That's so sad," Leah said.

"It is," Lance agreed. "So, is that everything?"

"Pretty much."

"Okay," Lance said, "That helps. Thank you, Leah. I'm sorry you had to look at all that."

"It's okay," she said, again thinking about how she needed to run her antivirus program, just to be sure. "What else can I do?"

"That's all for now, I think."

"And you still don't think this has anything to do with the kids committing suicide?"

A beat, then Lance said, "I don't see how. No."

"So, what does it mean?" she asked. "I mean, while the whole thing is gross and sad and all, it's not exactly illegal, right?"

"No, I guess not," Lance said. "But, honestly, I've got somebody right in front of me now that can probably help me figure that out."

Leah sat up in her bed. "One of the girls is with you right now?" she asked, marveling at the small twinge of completely irrational jealousy she felt stir in her gut (but hey, all those girls she'd seen online had been so pretty).

"Yes," Lance said. "So, I should probably go."

"Okay," she said.

"And, Leah, thank you again. I'm sorry I had to involve you in this, but I really appreciate the help."

They ended the call, and Leah sat quietly on her bed for a long time, thinking about a lot of things. Lance had said the suicides were not related to the webcam girls, and he was probably right—he did have a knack for this sort of thing. But Leah was still curious. And even if the two things weren't related—the girls and the suicides—it didn't mean she couldn't maybe find some more information online that could help. The problem was she didn't know where Lance was, which would make the Googling tougher to execute with any valuable results.

But then she remembered the online message boards. The ones with the lists of cities documenting where the webcam girls were selling their codes.

"He's in one of those," she said out loud. Then she opened her laptop and started to search, trying not to think about whether or not Lance would disapprove.

LANCE FLIPPED HIS PHONE CLOSED, SLIDING IT BACK INTO his pocket after his conversation with Leah. He looked at Diana across the table from him, her smooth skin, sparkling eyes, and blond hair all striking. There was no denying she was very pretty, and now Lance wondered how many men had scrolled across her picture on the website, had a similar thought (although with much more deviant intentions), and clicked to select her to fulfill their fantasies. But then he wondered if Diana was even *on* the website. Maybe there was some sort of hierarchy. Maybe you had to start low on the totem pole, sell the sodas on the street, doing the grunt work before you could earn your way to bedroom and...

Diana looked back at him, those eyes tainted with sadness.

I work and John pay. That was what she'd said to him, and now he understood more than he wanted to.

John.

John Doe.

Anonymous.

The men who visited the website paid their fee for the service provided. So why...

"Why did you say that if you go back to the house, the people there will make *you* pay more? You work for them, right? And the men online, they pay for the, uh, work you do? So, aren't you the one getting paid, at least a portion of it?"

If Diana was curious as to how Lance suddenly understood what it was she did for a living, she either didn't care or didn't feel they had the time for more questions. Instead, she said, "We go now? Leave from here? Please."

Lance shook his head. "No, not quite yet, I'm sorry. I will do my best to protect you, I promise, but you have to give me something."

At this phrase, Diana's face fell again, her eyes looking down with disappointment.

"No, no, not like that!" Lance said, waving his hands. "I mean, you need to tell me more information. Help me understand what's wrong. Why are you so afraid of the people you work for, and why did you have to run away in the middle of the night?"

Diana was quiet, fiddling with one of the used paper towels.

Lance reached across the table and took her hands in his, an act he performed gently, and was disappointed when he received no flash of memory, no instant download of events from Diana's past. He said, "Diana, tell me so I can help you."

Diana stared at Lance's big hands wrapped around hers and then looked up to meet his eyes. She must have seen something there, must have felt his honesty and kindness, because all at once Lance felt as if the air in the room had shifted, as if a bond of trust had finally been solidly formed.

Diana nodded once and started to tell him everything.

It was a story so sad, Lance wished he could go burn the house with the security cameras to the ground.

Though the story was sad, it was not an uncommon one, Lance was disheartened to realize. A tragic tale of one desperately seeking a better life, a happy home. Though her English was broken, and her story seemed to lack certain details Lance would have liked to have, he got the gist of it all.

Diana's family was poor, living in a country being torn apart by war and civil unrest. People were fleeing where they could, entire families uprooting and packing up what few possessions they had or could manage to take with them and heading off for anyplace that might be better than home. It was dangerous, and many were killed or turned away at borders, forced back to a life of poverty and potential death.

Diana's father was employed—one of a lucky few who'd been selected for factory work in the city—but the wages were small, and while his job did afford his family a small amount of stability in the uncertain times, it was only marginally better than others, and he dreamed of a better life for his family—particularly his daughter and wife.

One day at work, he learned of a new option. The grandest dream of all. Life in America.

He heard about a business (a scam was what it really was, though due to the man's excitement at the prospect, Lance thought, this didn't enter his mind, or he chose to not believe it) where a family could have their children smuggled out of the country, off to the safe haven that was the USA, and once there, the children would get a job and work, paying off the debt incurred for their transport, and also work to pay for the safe transport of their family at a later date. The only stipulation stated was the child must be at least fifteen years old.

(*I know it illegal*, Diana had said at this point, *Coming into country this way. But I not care. I just want to get away. Bring family with me. I would work to get them here.*)

There was an application process, a form to fill out with a

picture attached. Diana had been selected, and her family had cried with their happiness, the excitement of her getting out and one day bringing them, too. They all just had to survive a little longer.

The night she was to leave arrived, and she and her father went down to the docks in the city to board a boat—one of many on which she'd end up during her long journey across the Atlantic—there was a quick, forced goodbye as the men working hurried her along, below deck to join the others.

(*I think Papa knew something bad then*, Diana had said. *But it happen so fast.*)

And when she got below deck, clutching her one small bag she was allowed to bring, that was when Diana knew there was something bad, too.

All the passengers—all the children who'd been selected— were female.

And in a few weeks' time, each and every one of them would arrive on the shore of America and be forced into sexual servitude. Forced to continue their work with a threat that was twofold: not earning enough to bring their family to the Land of the Free, or being turned over to the police as an illegal and tossed in jail or deported back to their war-torn country, where they would live a life of poverty—if they lived at all.

They were slaves, plain and simple.

"But they lie," Diana said, her face flushing with anger after she'd finished her heartbreaking story. "They no bring families. Never. Nobody pay back debt. Always work."

Lance figured this much was the case. This was human trafficking, happening right here on US soil. These poor girls were *sold* by families duped into believing they were helping their children gain a better life. And they were likely never heard from again. And what choice did the girls have, once they discovered the truth? They were prisoners in a country that was not their own, threatened by things they didn't fully understand. And who could they turn to without fear of persecution?

"I don't know if my family still alive," Diana said, her voice growing quiet. "I think ... I think it easier for me if I think they dead. Or ... or if they think I dead. I never see them again."

Fresh tears welled in the girl's eyes, but she shook her head and held them back, wiping at the corners of her eyes with the paper towel.

Lance wanted to say that she shouldn't say things like that, that he was sure she'd see her family again. But he couldn't. It would be wrong. Deep down, he knew she was likely right. He couldn't help her with any of that. For now, all he could do was keep her safe and away from her captors.

"I'm so sorry," Lance said. It was all he could come up with.

Diana sniffled once, swallowed, and then looked at him with a face that was now extremely tired. The adrenaline of her escape from the house was apparently subsiding, and now it seemed as though she were drained of all her energy. Her shoulders slumped as she slid slowly down into the seat, her eyelids growing heavy.

"We go now?" she asked, her voice low.

Lance wished he could say yes. Wished he knew where to take her. But he couldn't. Not yet.

"No," he said. "Why don't you go upstairs and sleep. Get some rest and then we can figure this all out tomorrow."

She lifted her head to look at him, her eyes suddenly cautious again.

Lance held up his hands. "You're safe here," he said. "I promise." Then he stood from the table and held out a hand. Diana looked at it, and Lance could see her still debating whether any of this was some sort of trap. "You can trust me." Lance said. "In fact, I may be one of the only people who will ever say that to you who you can truly believe."

Lance didn't know if it was his words, or just Diana's exhaustion finally winning her over—*how long has it been since she's had a good night's sleep?*—but she did reach out and take his hand, letting him lead her up the staircase. At the top of the landing, Lance was hit with a small dilemma. He at first contemplated leading Diana to one of the other vacant rooms, giving her a space of her own, but he ultimately decided against it. He didn't want to abuse Loraine Linklatter's hospitality—he was, in fact, only paying for a single room—and on top of that, if Loraine discovered Diana in a room other than his own, that would only lead to more questions being asked, and Lance wasn't sure what he would be able to say as answers to any of them. He had to protect himself, and he promised Diana he would protect her as well.

As they stood there, Lance in the throes of his indecisiveness, another thought occurred to him. He thought again of the house with the cameras, the fence. He asked, "Diana, how did you get away? How did you escape?"

Diana's face showed no emotion. She simply said, "I did what had to."

So Lance, accepting this as all he needed to know, pushed open the door to his bedroom and led her inside. She did a cursory glance around the place, and Lance thought he saw a flicker of awe, an appreciation of fine surroundings. He pointed to the bed and said, "You can sleep there. But if you don't mind, I might steal a pillow so I can sleep on the floor and not have to use a stack of books."

He smiled, but Diana acted as though she hadn't heard the joke. Instead, she looked at him, then pointed to the bed. "Me?"

Lance nodded. "Yes. You. The bathroom is right down the

hall that way"—he pointed—"if you need it." But when he turned back, Diana was already across the room and standing next to the bed. She began stripping down, kicking off her shoes and socks and peeling off her sweatpants and sweatshirt, leaving her in nothing but her bra and panties. "Oh … okay," Lance said, looking away to give the girl her privacy, though she clearly didn't care. When he looked back, she was fully under the covers, her blond hair splayed across one of the pillows and one arm tucked beneath her head. Within seconds, she was asleep, the sound of her breathing becoming slow and steady.

Lance stood by the door and stared at her for a long time, his mind reeling as it tried to figure out what he was going to do.

"She's very pretty," Daisy said, suddenly standing next to him.

Lance, not surprised to see her, now that there was a new visitor, nodded his head. "She is," he said. "And she's had a very hard time."

Daisy looked on, seeming to think about this. "How?"

The innocence of children. Unafraid to ask questions. "Some people lied to her and took her from her family. They made her do a lot of things she didn't want to," Lance said, keeping things as G-rated as he could.

Daisy nodded her head, as if she understood everything. "That's sad," she said.

"Yes, it is."

"I hope she doesn't end up like the other ones. I like her."

Lance felt ice water rush through his veins. He spun and looked down at Daisy, who was looking back at him with wide eyes.

"You hope she doesn't end up like *who*?"

THEM
(III)

If they'd driven all the miles they'd added to the Element's odometer in a straight line, headed in one direction—north, south, east or west—they'd have crossed several states. But they hadn't gone in one direction. Instead, the Reverend, acting much like a bloodhound hot on the trail, had followed what few traces he could pick up from the boy, doing his best to give directions to the Surfer that would ultimately lead them to their prize. Because of this, they'd ended up zigzagging and backtracking and circling around to meaningless locations that might have been nothing more than where the boy had changed busses or stopped for a bite to eat.

The woman—the former Miss Sheila—had been a crucial piece of their puzzle. Not only had she verified the fact that the boy had been there—something the Reverend found suspiciously few people actually willing to do (he had a theory about this, something he figured the Surfer knew as well—opposing forces at work at a much higher level)—but because the boy had used his abilities to such an extent during his confrontation with the woman, the Reverend was able to pick up the scent much more clearly than he'd been able to for quite some time. Not since the night the boy's mother had died, followed by the town of Westhaven, which they knew had been his first stop.

But the boy was smart. He was not staying in one place for long, and if you tried to look for a pattern to his travel routes, you'd end up with something looking like one of those corkboards you always see in detective movies with pieces of string connecting various clues and leads—nothing but a spiderweb of confusion.

It had taken them weeks to finally leave the state of Virginia. But once they'd crossed the state line, the Reverend, while usually very patient, had perked up in a way that even the Surfer had noticed.

"Catchin' some good rays, man?" the Surfer had asked, leaned back in his seat with one tanned and muscular arm stretched out, gripping the wheel with loose fingers.

The Reverend had said that he was, in fact, catching some good rays, and had his partner take the next exit. They drove on in silence, which was both of their preferred way, the Reverend only speaking over the next few hours to tell the Surfer which roads to take. They left the interstate and bounced across a couple different highways before the Reverend took a deep breath and sat up straight in his seat.

"We're close," he said. "Right on top, in fact."

When the Surfer glanced at some of the road signs and saw where they were headed, he grinned and nodded his head. "Righteous."

As they'd gotten closer to the town, the Reverend had picked up on the feeling, the energy—or the *vibes*, as his partner would say. He'd trained himself onto it, inhaled it, followed it, giving the Surfer directions like a bloodhound leading a hunter.

They parked in the lot, watching as very few cars came and went, waiting for...

And then the Reverend saw him, walking along the front of the brightly lit building, and the rottenness of the man's soul was palpable.

"That's him," the Reverend said.

The Surfer tracked the man as he walked into the building. "Sure?"

The Reverend nodded.

He had a plan. And if knew the boy as well as he thought he did, it would certainly work.

[24]

LANCE COULD NOT SLEEP.

Not because of the huge daytime nap he'd taken after lunch, but because the information Daisy had just passed on to him was so jarring, such an unexpected revelation, he found himself doing nothing but pacing back and forth in the Boundary House's fancy kitchen, simultaneously trying to put together evidence that the theory he'd arrived at after Daisy had told him what she had was possible and also to convince himself it was ridiculous. *Impossible*. That he was a dog about to bark up the wrong tree.

Could he really accept this truth? And if he did, why hadn't he been able to figure this out more quickly on his own? The night he'd arrived at the Boundary House for the first time and had gotten the glimpse of Loraine Linklatter's past, why had the Universe decided to show him the visions of Daisy's life and eventual death, instead of...

I hope she doesn't end up like the others, Daisy had said.

The others, it turned out, had been other young people—somewhere around Lance's and Diana's age. A handful of them over the past year or so, Daisy had said. They stayed a night, sometimes two, she'd said. They didn't go out, didn't talk much, though Loraine tried to talk to them, Daisy said. She told Lance they'd all seemed very sad. She said she could feel it, like a chill that made her shiver.

"What happened to them?" Lance had asked, though he already knew the answer.

Daisy spoke quietly. "They're like me now."

And Lance's brain kicked into drive, a superhighway of information crisscrossing lanes and trying to find a destination.

He remembered what April, the girl working behind the counter at the donut shop, had told him when he'd asked about the suicides. *There's talk that there's somebody here who's helping them.*

And maybe giving them a nice place to stay in the process, Lance considered. With a fancy kitchen and bathroom and the best beds money could buy. A nice, peaceful send-off.

And as Lance let the acceptance of this idea begin to creep in, fully take hold, he nearly became dizzy with the idea that suddenly, he was no longer pacing in the kitchen of a comfortable bed-and-breakfast. He was pacing in the kitchen of a bed-and-breakfast that was also an assisted-suicide facility.

He had given money—his *mother's* money—to a woman who was helping people kill themselves. Perhaps sleeping in the exact same bed those poor kids had slept in.

Lance remembered the night he'd arrived in Sugar Beach, the way that the fire had seemed to summon him as he'd sat in the lifeguard stand. He remembered the way he'd seen the lamppost and the sign for the Boundary House and had had one of those gut feelings that the Universe had brought him to that exact spot for a reason. He'd assumed it was the right place to be to begin to solve the problem.

He'd never considered that the Boundary House was the actual problem to begin with.

But why? What was Loraine's motivation?

Daisy, he thought. Tragic events sometimes caused people to do tragic things. Terrible things. The death of a young child ... Lance could only imagine what sort of mental scarring that caused, what sort of logic might get broken. But still, he needed to talk to her.

Or just call the police, he reasoned. *Let them deal with it.*

But something held him back from that decision, aside from the usual inclination to avoid police whenever possible. Police asked lots of questions, and Lance was a guy who had a hard time answering questions about himself honestly. No, he had a feeling, too. It wasn't quite time. Plus, he had Diana asleep upstairs in his bed, and had made a promise to her he'd keep her safe. He'd talk to Loraine first.

His cell phone buzzed in his pocket, loud enough in the silent kitchen that Lance nearly screamed in surprise. He fished in the pocket of his shorts and pulled the phone free, checking the screen and seeing Leah's name. He smiled. Despite it all, he smiled. He could use a friend right now.

"Hi," he said. "I'm glad you called."

"You're in Sugar Beach, Maryland, aren't you?"

Lance leaned against the counter, silent for a long time, checking the digital clock on the front of the high-tech fridge and seeing that it was nearly two in the morning. He had no idea how long he'd been pacing back and forth, how long he'd disappeared into his own thoughts.

"Lance?" Leah asked. Her voice was firm, matter-of-fact.

What could he say? She'd figured it out, and he would not lie. She knew the risks. He'd told her as best he could. Yet still, she'd persisted. He realized quickly that it was his own doing, telling her about both the girls selling soda *and* the kids committing suicide. He knew enough about the Internet to realize she'd probably figured out his location in less time than it would have taken him to finish a cup of coffee.

"*Lance?*"

He would not lie.

"Yes," he said. "You're correct."

She let out a sigh that whispered in his ear. "See, now was that really so hard?"

Lance said nothing. Waited.

"Listen," Leah said, "since you're handicapped with that inferior technology you call a cell phone, and I wasn't sure how much you'd been able to find out about the people committing suicide. I thought I'd check into it for you, you know, to try and help some more."

Lance slid into the breakfast nook, taking the same side as when he'd sat with Diana earlier as she'd eaten her late dinner. "You didn't have to do that, Leah. You'd already done more than I should have asked of you." *Clearly, since you've Sherlock Holmes'd your way into figuring out where I am*, Lance thought but did not say.

She waited a beat, then said, "You know, you're right. What was I thinking? I forgot you prefer to save the world all by your lonesome. And, you know what, it's past my bedtime, so I'll go ahead—"

"Please tell me what you found out," Lance blurted, feeling a rush of heat to his face. *She wants to help, Lance. You don't get to make that decision for her.* "I'm sorry," he said. He took a deep breath. "Really. I ... I do appreciate you helping. And right now I could definitely use it."

She pushed on. "Okay, good. That's better. You're welcome." She cleared her throat as if about to give a speech. "Now, I don't want you thinking I went and solved this for you, so don't get too excited, but I got the gist of what's going on and discovered something kinda interesting that ties into what you told me earlier.

"Five people have been found dead of an apparent suicide in Sugar Beach over the past year or so, both male and female, ages ranging from eighteen to twenty-three. All of their families said basically the same thing: they had no idea their child was even unhappy, and certainly not on the brink of suicide."

Lance thought about the actor Robin Williams—how he'd made the entire world laugh and had seemed like the most care-free guy in the world on the outside and had ended his own life. *Does anyone really know anything about anyone else? We all have demons.*

"The oldest one was the first," Leah said. "A girl from the University of Maryland. She'd gotten a master's degree in biology and was working on a PhD."

"Wow," Lance said.

"I know. Just like the parents said, they had no idea. But anyway, the rest followed after her, staggered every few months. Nobody was too certain why Sugar Beach was suddenly the hot spot for this sort of thing, but two of the articles I read—ones by some bigger publications, I guess with better resources and more motivated journalists—hinted at some message boards on the Dark Web for folks looking for help with going through with their planned suicides."

"Dark Web?" Lance asked.

"It's like a secret Internet," Leah said. "For bad stuff, mostly. You see it a lot in movies and TV, but it's real. Instead of shopping on Amazon for a pack of socks, you go to the Dark Web and shop for stolen credit card numbers."

"Please tell me you didn't try to find this website."

Leah made a dismissive sound. "You kidding me? I'm not *that* dumb."

"You don't know how, do you?"

"Shut up."

"Leah..."

"Okay, I get it. Don't worry. I'll stick to the boring regular Internet."

"Thank you."

"*Anyway*, my guess is, if there's really somebody in Sugar Beach who is helping these people end their lives, they're on that message board, trolling around looking for new ... is *customers* the right word?"

"You think they're *paying* for this?"

Leah was quiet for a minute, thinking. "Yes, I think they might be. I mean, seems like an odd hobby, don't you think? No, I think there's profit here somewhere."

Lance looked at the fancy refrigerator. Expensive, had to be.

He wasn't going to tell Leah he thought he knew who was helping with these suicides, and he certainly wasn't going to tell her he was actually only one flight of stairs away from said person. But he did have one more question. "Leah, did these articles say how these kids took their lives?"

"Drugs," she said instantly. "They overdosed on some wild concoction of pills, so says the medical examiner. Same thing for all five."

Lance thought about how he'd first assumed the girls selling the sodas had been drug-related. Right idea, wrong side of the coin.

"And there's one more thing," Leah said. "All five kids' bodies were found in a similar spot. Right on the beach, like they'd washed up onto shore."

Lance was quiet for a long time. Putting pieces together.

His silence must have been telling.

"This all means something to you, doesn't it?" Leah asked. "You're too quiet, like you're working it all out in your head."

She knows me well, Lance thought. Incredible, really, when you considered how little time they'd actually spent together.

"Yes," he said.

"Yes, what?"

"It all means something. I think I know who's profiting from these kids' mental illness."

Now it was Leah who was quiet. Then she asked, "What are you going to do about it?"

"I don't know yet."

And to change the subject, Lance told Leah what he'd learned about Diana and the other girls that worked for the website Leah had told him about. When he was finished, Leah said, "That's so incredibly sad." She made a disgusted sound that reverberated across the digital line. "God, sometimes I really hate this world we live in."

Lance said nothing.

"So what are you going to do with her?" Leah asked. "I mean, do you think those people will come looking for her? They have to, right? If they think she'll expose their whole operation. I mean, the list of illegal things they're involved in is a mile long—underage sex-workers are only the tip of it."

Lance suddenly had a craving for coffee. A caffeine jolt so his brain could keep up.

He settled for saying, "I don't know what I'm doing about any of it, but..."

"But what?"

"But whatever's going to happen, it's got to be now, and it's got to be fast."

Leah said, "Well, that doesn't sound good."

"I'm playing two against one here," Lance said. "Not impossible, but no room for error. One slipup and I lose. I've got to play smart."

Leah made another of those disgusted sounds, though this

one was less imposing. "You know, Mr. Hero, you could just, I don't know, walk away from it all. Nobody's making you do any of this. There's a billion people out there, and every single one of them needs some sort of help. You can't save them all."

Lance said nothing. He understood her frustration. It was coming from the same place, fed by the same fear and concern that had caused him to shut her out for so long after he'd left Westhaven. She cared about him. Didn't want to see him hurt ... or worse.

But every time Lance found himself considering running away, abandoning somebody in need of his help, he would see his mother's face as she lay dying on the ground. The greatest sacrifice he would ever know.

The line was quiet for a long time. Finally, Leah said, "Lance?"

"Yes?"

"Play smart, okay?"

[25]

LANCE FOUND A FRENCH PRESS IN THE CABINET AND A container of ground beans next to it. He filled the kettle with water and waited for it to heat, scooped coffee into the French press and finished the job. Pulled a mug from a different shelf in the same cabinet and filled it to the rim. No need to leave room for cream or sugar. Black was just fine. He took a sip. Hot and strong. Good.

He carried it down the short hallway and to the front door. He unlocked the door and had it halfway open before considering whether or not there might be an alarm system. He might be adept at helping solve crimes, but as a thief he would be lousy. No alarm blared and no lights started flashing, and after waiting a minute to see if Loraine Linklatter was going to come running to the top of the stairs with a baseball bat or shotgun in her hands, Lance figured he was in the clear. He closed the door and went to sit on one of the porch swings.

He sat, alone in the dark with his thoughts and the salty air and the cool, misty breeze coming in from over the dunes. He used the heels of sneakers to rock the porch swing back and forth, back and forth, matching his own internal decision making process.

Confront Loraine Linklatter ... or not?

Part of him, despite his outrage that somebody could be so cavalier with a human life, especially one that was not their own, was focusing on Diana and the hell she'd escaped from, and how he could help with that. It was the more tangible scenario, and he was beginning to form an idea of what he needed to do—both to deliver Diana to safety (to the best of his ability, anyway) and to put an end to the people who'd wronged her and her family.

But the other part of him kept coming back to five dead kids. All adults by age, sure. But kids, all the same. Young people—at least one well educated—with their entire lives before them. No doubt they'd needed help. But not of the type they'd received. They'd needed help to live, not to die. Lance considered that just as sinful as murder—as might a court of law, he guessed.

Plus, there was Daisy. He still couldn't figure how she fit into all this. She'd told him about the kids all staying at the Boundary House, but that couldn't be her only purpose. Couldn't be why she'd been waiting all this time for somebody —*him*—to show up.

She still needs me, he reasoned. *Or she needs a reason to move on.*

Could he help with that? He didn't know.

He sipped his coffee and looked at the ceramic frog by the door. "You've probably been here a while," Lance said. "Any opinion on the situation?"

The frog was silent, but Lance read plenty into the way those large eyes seemed to stare at him. "Yeah, you're right," Lance said. "I know."

He sighed and stood from the porch swing. Gulped down

the rest of his coffee and patted the frog on its head before pushing through the door, back into the house.

Loraine Linklatter stood in the foyer, robe cinched tight, a small pistol clutched in her right hand. It was pointed directly at Lance's chest.

Lance held up his hands and offered timidly, "Um ... don't shoot?"

"Oh, it's just you," Loraine said. "I heard somebody on the porch, but I figured you'd be in with your girl." She kept the gun trained on him, though not as assuredly. After a moment she shook her head, as if she'd finally gotten fed up with it all. "Who are you?" she asked.

Lance said nothing.

"I mean, I know you're Lance," Loraine said, waving the gun in a hurry-it-along gesture. "What I mean is, *who are you? Why are you really here?*"

"Can you put the gun down first?" Lance said, his mind whirring into gear, trying to find a balance of survival mode and how to capitalize on this opportunity to get answers from Loraine Linklatter. Because clearly whatever he was meant to do with her, it was going to happen right now.

Or she would shoot him. There was always that option, Lance supposed. All he had to defend himself with was a coffee mug with a spit's worth of liquid in the bottom. Not great odds. Okay, next-to-impossible odds, and Lance never was much of a gambler.

His silence causes her to press on, more aggravated. "Whatever you're up to, you need to tell me. It's my right to know, being you're staying in *my* home. I'll kick you and your little girlfriend upstairs right out of here, don't think I won't."

"Why do you think I'm up to something?" Lance asked.

She rolled her eyes, jutted the gun forward. "I wasn't born yesterday, Lance."

Lance considered this statement. Then considered this: If Loraine Linklatter was, in fact, running some sort of assisted-suicide business by lurking in the message boards of some secret Internet that Leah didn't even know how to access, *and* had managed to keep it all a secret up until this point, there was no denying that she was intelligent. Sometimes Lance marveled over how some of the most clever people were criminals. He often wondered what sort of things they could have achieved if they'd used their powers for good, so to speak.

"I had a feeling about you," Loraine said. "As soon as I saw you last night on the porch. I couldn't make heads or tails of it— still can't, actually—but there was something there ... something *in the air* with you. Like, well, to be honest, I had this odd sense that you were here to help."

Lance jumped at this. "Help with what?"

Loraine, who'd seemed like maybe she was easing back into her normal self, floated in thoughtfulness for just a moment before her eyes snapped back to attention and her stare hardened. "You tell me, Lance. I'll ask again: Why are you here?"

After some quick deliberation, Lance decided his best defense might be a strong offense. After all, he'd told Leah he was going to have to move fast, whatever he did. Now seemed like as good a time as any.

He sighed, as if now he was tired of the game. "Okay," he started. "How about we trade?"

Loraine's eyes narrowed in confusion. "Trade what?"

"Answers," Lance said. "I'll tell you why I'm here, and you can tell me why you're luring kids to your posh B&B and helping them kill themselves before you dump their bodies on the beach." And then out of nowhere, anger flooded out of him.

"How about you tell me exactly why you feel like you have the right to *ruin* the lives of *five different families*?"

He'd hissed these last words louder than he'd wanted. Diana was still upstairs asleep, and he didn't want to get her involved in this. They might be fleeing from here in a matter of minutes anyway, depending on how Loraine Linklatter reacted, but for now, it was better if she stayed where she was. Oblivious and uninformed and not a liability.

Lance was ready. He gripped the coffee mug tightly in his hand, with the ridiculous notion he could beat the odds and use it as a weapon if need be. A projectile, a distraction, anything to keep him from taking a bullet. His body was wound tight, his muscles tense and ready to spring into action—either directly at Loraine, hoping to knock the gun from her hand as they collide, or retreat out the door behind him. Open spaces were always nice in a fight, Lance had found.

But instead of anger, instead of retaliation or any other intensely charged reaction, Lance was surprised to see Loraine Linklatter lower her weapon and meet his gaze with eyes that looked as though they finally understood.

"Are you a private investigator? Did one of the families hire you?"

Is she actually going to admit it? Just like that?

Lance shook his head. "No," he said. "I'm just a guy passing through."

Now Loraine shook her head in response. "No," she said. "You're more than that."

Lance nodded. "I am. But that's all I'm telling you for now. Why are you killing kids? Why shouldn't I call the police right now?"

And suddenly Loraine looked very, very tired. She sighed, heavily, and with it, Lance sensed some sort of relief, as though a great ruse had finally been revealed, and Loraine could stop playing the game. "You could," she said. "Call the police, I mean. I am guilty, in a sense."

"In a sense?"

"Yes," Loraine said. "But not the way you think."

Now it was Lance's eyes that narrowed, skeptical. "Enlighten me, please."

Loraine took a long time considering this. She sighed heavily again, and in the dim foyer lighting, Lance could see the glistening of tears welling up in her eyes. She forced them back and asked, "How did you know?"

The truth would only upset her more. Lance shrugged. "It's just what I do."

It was a bad answer that wasn't really an answer at all, but Loraine accepted it. She nodded, then turned and started down the hallway. "Come on," she said. "I'll make some tea and I'll tell you. After, you can decide what you want to do."

Lance, who was fully aware that Loraine Linklatter still held a gun in her hand, a gun that she'd continued to point at him even after she'd learned he was not a burglar or other home invader of the traditional sense, knew his only option was to follow her.

He decided not to tell her he was more of a coffee guy.

[26]

LORAINE LINKLATTER MADE HERSELF SOME TEA. LANCE refilled his coffee mug with what was left in the French press and tried to wrap his head around the fact that the two of them were acting like they were an old couple getting ready to start a book club meeting, instead of one of them keeping a pistol within easy reach and the other trying to lay blame on them for causing five innocent people to lose their lives. It seemed incredibly civilized, entirely too implausible.

The last time Lance had faced down somebody he was accusing of murder, it had been in a dark basement, and a shotgun had been involved. The perpetrator had not taken the accusation well at all. Weapons had been fired that night, blood had been shed. Police had arrived. An ambulance and paramedics had been needed. Lance had escaped by a hair on his head.

So, being invited to share a warm beverage and discuss the way of things after calling somebody out on their crimes was something Lance found himself increasingly uneasy with.

Unless...

Unless I'm wrong about her, Lance thought.

191

Loraine slid into the breakfast nook and Lance stayed where he was, leaning against the counter, next to the fancy fridge.

"Would you like to sit?" Loraine asked.

"I'm good here, thanks," Lance said. "No offense, but as a moving target, I'll be a lot harder to hit if you decide our talking has gone ... not the way you'd like it to."

"I'm not going to shoot you, Lance. I'm not a..." A pause. "I won't hurt you. Like I said, I'll tell you what I know, and you can decide the rest."

Lance said nothing, and he did not move. He sipped his coffee.

Loraine nodded, as if understanding completely. "I'm sorry," she said. "Really. About the gun. I just ... I heard the door open, even though I knew I had locked it, so I just panicked a bit —habit of a woman living by herself, I guess—and then I saw somebody on the porch and, I guess, once I saw it was you, I just sort of ... I just needed to know what was going on. I guess ... I just knew it was all coming to an end."

"*What* was coming to an end?" Lance moved down the counter, a bit closer to the breakfast nook. In the glow of the small light hanging above the table, Loraine Linklatter's face looked calmer than Lance had ever seen it, even more so than when he'd watched her doing yoga. "I'm not sure if you're doing it on purpose, but you're being incredibly cryptic, if I might say so. And that's coming from a guy who ... well, let's just say I know how to say as little as possible when need be."

"Well, there you go. Something we have in common." Loraine smiled at him, and Lance realized what she was doing.

"You're stalling," he said. "Why?" And he had a terrible thought that whatever Loraine Linklatter was involved in, maybe there was a connection to the house with the security cameras and the girls selling sodas. Maybe she'd recognized Diana and had played dumb, but then called somebody and asked them if they knew one of their girls was out shacking up with the new guy in town, off the clock. Maybe they were on the way right now, to pick up their product and take care of the loose end. Him. He could practically hear the engine of the black Excursion pulling up to the curb.

"Because," Loraine said. "Because it's *hard*." And then the tears came. Loud and heavy and unabashed. "I just ... I couldn't take it anymore!" Loraine said in between gasps of air as she continued to sob. She'd gone from zero to sixty in two seconds, and Lance stood by, confused as ever as the second person in one night had broken down hysterically in front of him.

Loraine cried for what felt like forever, and Lance pulled a paper towel from the roll and handed it to her. He was getting good at that. She took it, thanking him, and slowly got herself under control again. When her breathing had returned to normal, she took a long sip of her tea, as if it were a swig of whisky to calm her nerves.

"I used to be a psychologist," she said, wiping her mouth with the napkin. "Did you know that? No, of course you didn't," Loraine said, chuckling. "How could you?"

Lance said nothing.

"But, yes, I was. PhD from UNC, a couple of papers published. Decent career. Was even considering starting my own practice, but then we got pregnant and nothing seemed to matter but family. We moved here, we had Daisy, and everything was ... perfect." She closed her eyes, remembering, and she smiled. "It was perfect, Lance."

She opened her eyes. Stared down into her tea. "But then Daisy got sick, and..."

Fresh tears trickled down her cheek.

"And then everything *wasn't* perfect," she said. She wiped at the tears with the back of her hand and looked at Lance. "It's funny, you know? All my education, all my training, all my *years* of devoting my time to helping other people deal with their demons, the monkeys on their backs, the skeletons in their closets and every other metaphor you can throw around ... and I didn't know how to help myself." She shook her head, slowly. "I *couldn't* help myself, and I couldn't save my little girl."

Lance said nothing.

Loraine was quiet then, for a very long time. Lance set his coffee mug on the counter, put his hands in his pockets and waited. Finally, Loraine looked up at him. "You're here to find out what happened to those kids, right?"

"I want to know who's helping them," Lance said. "And if you're not that person, I think now is the time to let me know."

Loraine shook her head. "Did you listen to what I just told you? I was a *psychologist*. My *job* was to help people, including those who dealt with depression and anxiety and, yes, entertained suicidal thoughts. And after ... after Daisy, how could you think I would encourage somebody to end their life?"

Lance shrugged. "All I know is that they stayed here, under your roof, and then they died."

"You still haven't told me how you found that out," Loraine said.

"You're right," Lance said. "I haven't."

"Somebody told you?"

"Yes?"

"Who?"

Lance said, "I can't tell you. And you wouldn't believe me if I did."

Loraine shook her head. "Now who's being cryptic?"

Lance said nothing. The air in the room seemed to shift, and with it came an almost imperceptible feeling of unease. It was so faint, even Lance had a hard time picking up its traces. But it was there. Something was stirring, but he wasn't sure what.

Loraine let out a heavy sigh that sounded as though she

were releasing a decade's worth of frustration. Her head dropped, her chin almost touching her chest. She spoke, barely a whisper. "*So tired of the lies*," she said. "*So tired of lying to myself.*"

"Ma'am?" Lance said, taking a small step closer.

Loraine raised her head, looked at him. She asked, "Do you have any idea, Lance, what it's like to walk around in life carrying such an enormous, terrible secret that the entire world would look at you differently if they ever learned the truth?"

Lance answered honestly. "Yes, ma'am. I do, actually."

Loraine acted as though she hadn't even heard him. "A secret so disgusting, so vile and unthinkable that they'd hang you in the center of town if it were still acceptable? Even if they have no idea—*no idea!*—what it was like, how much we suffered, how hard we tried! Oh, they would say they'd never be able to do such a thing, I'm sure. They'd say all the right things and act like they all would have been *stronger*, but it's bullshit. *Bullshit.* If they haven't lived it, they'll never know."

The stirring in the air crept closer. Lance could feel it growing. He didn't like it. He looked around the kitchen. Expecting what, he didn't know. But he knew this feeling—if not the specifics, the underlying idea.

Something bad.

"Ma'am? I think maybe—"

"I bought the drugs from him," Loraine said, cutting Lance off. "There, you wanted a name, here it is. Jerry. *Jerry* is the one selling the kids the drugs they're using to kill themselves. He calls it the Emergency Exit package, the sick bastard."

And then a fresh wave of tears was washing down her face and causing her breath to stutter and words to come out in garbled, rushed syllables. "I ... it's my fault. I had him ... I had him start ... making it. I was ... his first ... customer."

And Lance's heart dropped to his gut. More pieces fell into place.

Loraine didn't even bother with wiping the tears or the snot from her face. She looked Lance fully in the eyes and spoke with an eerie coldness in between breaths. "There are security cameras in the bus station. I should have known that, but I wasn't thinking. He said I'm on video, talking to him both times —once for the initial request, and again for the pickup. Stupid of me. So stupid. *He* knew, though. *He* knew exactly what he was doing. I found out later he never deals directly from the station. He always plans different places, different times. But he saw an opportunity in me. He used the footage to blackmail me. I never told him why I wanted what I did from him, but after what happened, the timing of it all—again, I should have been smarter about it, not that it would have changed anything in the long run —he put two and two together and figured out what I'd done. It's the curse of the small town." She shook her head and gave off a sad laugh. "God, I was so stupid in my grief. But, that's how the Boundary House became the last place these kids would ever sleep before Jerry delivered his Emergency Exit and they'd walk off to the beach together. He needed a safe place to make his deal, and I needed my secret kept."

Lance did not want to accept the truth he was hearing. The horror of it was...

"So," Loraine said, "if you want the person who's actually feeding the pills to them, your man is Jerry. He's the janitor at the bus station, but that's just a ruse to cover his real income." Loraine shrugged with shoulders that had absolutely given up hope. "What better place, right?"

And Lance was transported back to the very first moment after his arrival in Sugar Beach. The janitor in the men's room, staring at him and asking, "Are you here to die?"

It all made sense. Horrible, tragic sense. The man Lance

had been trying to find from the moment he'd realized there was a problem in Sugar Beach was the very first person who'd spoken to him.

But right now, there was something else. Something that was making his stomach churn and his insides boil. There was only one thing Loraine Linklatter could have done that would have been so terrible, so universally condemned, that she would stand quietly by and allow a man to run a suicide factory out of her home.

"What did you do?" Lance said, his voice firm and deep. He needed to hear her say it. It was impossible to accept it based only on assumption.

She'd purchased the Emergency Exit from Jerry the janitor, and *she* was still alive. But there was somebody else in the Boundary House who wasn't.

Loraine took a deep breath. Closed her eyes, squeezing out final tears. When she opened them, she said, "I killed my daughter. I couldn't watch her suffer anymore, so I killed her."

And before Lance could even fully process the words, the air came alive with a hum, there was a rush of pressure that Lance knew only he could feel, a buzzing like the sound of a thousand bees rushing past.

Evil.

And Lance saw what would happen a fraction of a second before it did. Not enough time for him to reach Loraine Linklatter before she picked up the pistol from the table and then put the barrel to her temple and pulled the trigger.

[27]

LORAINE LINKLATTER'S BODY HAD SLUMPED FORWARD, bent in half at the waist, torso and head resting atop the table. Her neck was bent awkwardly. The tiny black hole where the bullet had entered looked innocent enough, could maybe even be mistaken for a mole at the right distance and in the right lighting. But there was nothing innocent about the blood and brain matter and bits of Loraine Linklatter's skull that had exploded from the opposite side of her head and splattered against the wall of the breakfast nook. Her eyes were half-open still, lifeless. But Lance thought he saw accusation there, boring into him. *Look what you made me do, Lance.*

He shook his head. *No,* he thought. *You did this to yourself.*

All of this—the gunshot, the expulsion of brain and blood and life, Lance's passing moment of guilt—happened in the span of only three of four seconds. And after that, Lance's survival instinct took over, his mind shifting into damage control mode.

The gun had fallen from Loraine Linklatter's hand and scattered across the kitchen floor. Lance gave it only a cursory glance, not daring to touch it. He didn't plan on being anywhere near this place when the police came, but when they did, the last thing he wanted was his fingerprints on a weapon.

And the police would come. Surely a neighbor had heard the gunshot. It had sounded like a cannon firing in the confines of the kitchen, and Lance's ears were still ringing, like tiny sirens sounding off in his head as he tried to think.

Diana, he thought. *We've got to get out of here.*

He ran from the kitchen and down the hall, bounding up the stairs two at a time. He pushed against his bedroom door and flung it open, rocking it on its hinges, the door slamming against the wall hard enough that the doorknob punctured a hole in the drywall. Diana was sitting bolt upright in the bed, the covers pulled up to her chin, her eyes wide, like white saucers in the darkness. Lance flipped on the light switch and raised his hands.

"It's just me," he said. "We have to go. Like, right now. Get dressed." He walked around the bed and grabbed his backpack, slinging the straps over his shoulders.

Diana nodded and leapt from the bed, no questions asked. Lance guessed that when you came from a country at war, you grew used to this sort of thing. He watched as she quickly dressed, again showing no signs of modesty as she stood half-naked, pulling on her sweatpants. Once she'd finished, pulling on her shoes, she began walking toward him and finally asked, "I heard gunshot?"

"Yes," Lance said, taking her by the hand and leading her out onto the landing.

"You hurt?" Diana asked, letting him lead her.

"No. Not me. Loraine ... the woman who you saw earlier. She's dead."

Diana said nothing. She asked no more questions.

Lance had told her she could trust him. Apparently she was taking that to heart.

Which was a fact that only made Lance want to succeed in helping rescue her even more. Her blind faith in him was worth nothing if he could not deliver on his promise to keep her safe.

He'd started working on a plan for her earlier as he'd sat on the porch, and he was fairly certain it was the best he could offer her, given both of their circumstances. But now that plan was being forced into action faster than he'd anticipated. The biggest issue was time. How much of it they had, he didn't know. But between Diana's people potentially looking to reclaim her, and the authorities possibly being alerted at this very moment about the sound of gunfire coming from the Boundary House Bed & Breakfast, Lance figured it was safer to bet on less of it rather than more.

Which brought to light the issue of transportation. He needed to get Diana to the bus station, and he had to do it fast. Loraine Linklatter might have a car somewhere, but even if Lance could find the keys, he didn't figure getting caught driving the stolen car of a dead woman would help him in any way at all.

But Lance realized he had another option. One single other person in Sugar Beach who might have both the ability and the desire to risk themselves to help him.

He pulled his cell phone from his pocket and found Todd's number. Pressed Send.

Todd picked up on the third ring, and Lance wasted no time, identifying himself and then giving Todd a very simple request. "You can't ask questions, and you can't tell anybody what you're doing, but if you really want to do some good in this world and help me with something that is much bigger than either of us, come pick me up at the Boundary House right now. As fast as you can. I need a ride to the bus station. Can you do that?"

The line was quiet for what felt like an eternity, and Lance was certain he'd been wrong about the guy, that he was more talk than walk. But then Todd said, "My roommate has a car. It's a piece of shit, but it runs. I can be there in ten."

"Thank you," Lance said.

He led Diana down the steps and into the foyer, standing by the window next to the front door and waiting for a piece of shit to pull up to the curb, hoping beyond hope it would arrive before any police. He considered taking Diana and going to wait in the little park across the street, just to get out of the house, but decided to stay put. Ten minutes felt like a very long time.

And all Lance could see in his mind was Loraine Linklatter's lifeless body slumped against the kitchen table, her half-open eyes staring at him while her blood dried in dark, rusty splotches on the wall.

Lance gave Todd credit on two counts: he was right on time, pulling up to the curb outside the Boundary House almost exactly ten minutes after they'd ended their phone call, and the car he was driving was, in fact, a piece of shit. As Lance opened the house's door and he and Diana walked down the porch steps and through the gate, Lance thought the thing Todd was driving looked more like something you'd see out in the dirt at a monster truck rally, sitting in a line with other cars put out to pasture, waiting for their turn to get squished under tires the size of a single-story home. The muffler was badly damaged—or missing, Lance reasoned—and the car made just enough noise that Lance figured there might be one hard-of-hearing citizen of Sugar Beach that would *not* hear them make their middle-of-the-night escape. So much for stealth and discretion.

Lance pulled the handle to open the rear door, hinges screaming for a drop of WD-40, and waved for Diana to get in.

Then he opened the front passenger door and tossed his backpack into the floorboard before folding himself into the seat. The car smelled badly of cigarette smoke and marijuana, which instantly gave Lance a sick feeling in his stomach and the start of small headache behind his eyes, but he took solace in the fact that he wouldn't have to be inside the vehicle long. He looked at Todd, who was staring into the rearview mirror, looking at Diana like he was seeing a celebrity up close. Clearly recognizing her as one of the girls with the coolers, from around town.

"She needs help," Lance said. "All those girls do. But right now, all I'm worried about is her. We have to go."

"What happened?" Todd asked. "Why the hurry? Is somebody looking for her?"

"Yes," Lance said, keeping Loraine Linklatter out of it for now. "But, please, don't ask questions. We need to go, now. Something happened, and they might be here soon."

"Who?"

He's not listening very well, Lance thought. Though he couldn't blame the guy.

"I don't know, honestly. But whoever does show up, it won't end well for her ... or me, maybe. We can't afford the risk."

Todd took his eyes away from the rearview and turned to look at Lance. The two men locked eyes for a moment, and both of them seemed to circle back to the understanding they'd discovered in the laundromat earlier; they could trust each other. Todd nodded and put the car into gear, driving forward and pulling out onto Sand Dollar Road.

"Bus station, right?" Todd asked, sitting up straight in the driver's seat, both hands gripping the wheel and looking like he was ready to pull off high-speed precision maneuvers if it came to that.

"Yes, please," Lance said.

Todd nodded again. And again and again. As if Lance's answer made more sense than anything he'd ever heard before.

"I knew there was something wrong," he said. "I mean, I think a lot of folks did, but, like, hey ... what could we do?"

Lance said nothing.

"Was it drugs?" Todd asked. "Sex? Were they prostitutes?"

"You realize she speaks English and is sitting two feet away from you, right?" Lance said. Then he turned to the backseat and said, "Diana, this is Todd. He's good. Trust me."

Diana's eyes flicked to Todd from the backseat, then back to Lance, nodding once. "Todd ... nice to meet."

"Uh, yeah, you too, Diana. Glad to help," Todd said, glancing back at her quickly in the rearview one time before returning his eyes to the road. Then he added, "I'm sorry. About ... well, anything. I'm sorry."

They rode in silence from that point on, nothing but the sound coming from the barely-a-muffler disturbing the night. At this hour, most things on Sand Dollar Road were shutting down or already had. Signage was turned off and doors were locked. Traffic was nearly nonexistent. The fun and tourist dollars on hold until morning. As they slowly made their way down the road, Todd obeying traffic laws as if he were taking the DMV behind-the-wheel exam, Lance considered his options, knowing he'd have to make a choice very, very soon.

Option one, he could leave—not with Diana, but tonight. Different bus, different destination. Because there was no way he could go where he was going to send her. Not yet, and maybe never again. Lance knew there was no way he could single-handedly run a rescue operation for all the girls who sold the sodas and did all the other things they were being forced to do on the website, but he had an idea that the other person his plan was going to rely on might be able to pull it off. This person had the right sort of connections, so he could get Diana out of town before somebody else found her, and then let the rest of the pieces fall where they might.

You can't save them all, Lance.

But he could save the one riding in the car with him.

Option two, he could stay in Sugar Beach a little while longer. Because, much like some of the spirits he'd come across in this life, Lance felt weighed down with what he could only call unfinished business. There were too many other loose ends, things that if he left Sugar Beach tonight, he'd always wonder what more he could have done. Wonder who he'd failed.

Could he put an end to Jerry the janitor's drug dealing, or at least his luring of those in desperate need of mental healthcare and offering them a terrible way out—his Emergency Exit? A call to the police would do it, maybe. Anonymous, of course. Lance figured that if he gave the authorities enough of the pieces, they'd be able to put the puzzle together. And then Jerry the janitor would be at the mercy of the judicial system. Lance knew he had to remove his anger from the equation, because frankly, nothing short of death and dismemberment seemed adequate for Jerry.

Lance also thought of the kids on the beach, and how something seemed to be tugging at him to see them one more time. Why, he wasn't sure. Maybe one of them had more sage advice to offer. Maybe just to say goodbye.

And lastly, but maybe most importantly, he thought of Daisy. Wondered what she was doing right now, if she was standing alone in the kitchen of the Boundary House, staring at the body of her dead mother, more confused than ever before.

He wondered if she'd ever find her way out, or if she'd stay there forever, stuck in a house that was no longer hers, with nobody to show her the way home.

Todd pulled into the bus station's parking lot and then parked as close as he could to the building. Lance hadn't even realized they'd come so far, had gotten lost in his own mind. "Need me to come in with you?" Todd asked.

Lance threw open the door and thought for a moment it was going to swing all the way open and slam into the front side of the car. "No, I think we'll..." And then he stopped, an instant shift in decision. "Actually, yeah. Come on in, please."

The three of them made the short walk across the parking lot, Todd in the lead, Diana behind him, wrapping her arms around herself against the night's chilled air, and Lance bringing up the rear, his head swiveling across the lot, looking for any sign of somebody approaching. He saw nothing but a few empty cars scattered in various parking spots, and two busses idling along the departure lane, purring with a low rumble. *Good*, Lance thought. *She'll go out on one of those.* He'd feared that because of the hour, there'd be a chance Diana wouldn't be able to leave Sugar Beach until morning. Which, Lance realized, was fast approaching.

He was very thankful for the nap he'd accidentally taken earlier. Though by now he knew it was no accident.

The inside of the bus station looked just as it had before. The lights were bright and the white flooring was clean and smelling of disinfectant. Lance did a quick survey of the rows of seating and found only two people there, one man and one woman sitting three rows apart from each other and both looking down at the screens of their smartphones. The man paid them no attention, captivated by what was on his screen. The woman, wearing tight black jeans and a Sugar Beach hoodie, managed to look up as Lance led his group to the ticket window, her eyes going down the line. She lingered on them a little too long, Lance felt. But he was probably just being paranoid.

At the ticket window, Barb, the woman who'd been there before, the one who'd been flinging colored fruit around on her iPad screen and had told Lance that he was loved, was gone.

She'd been replaced by a rough-looking man dressed in heavy work pants and boots—which he had on the counter, just like the woman with the iPad had—and a long-sleeved knitted shirt. Scruffy beard and long hair curling around his ears. Toothpick in his mouth, which he was rolling back and forth while he flipped through the latest Cabela's catalogue. When he saw them approach the window, he snapped into action, polite and full of enthusiasm in the way people might be when they were new to a job and didn't quite know what they were doing yet.

Lance asked the man which of the two busses outside could get a passenger to Hillston, Virginia the quickest. The man, saying "Yessir. Of course, sir," turned to a computer hidden away on the corner of the desk and slowly searched the screen with the mouse cursor like he was looking at a *Where's Waldo* book. He found what he was looking for and then used the index fingers on both his hands to peck out some words and press the Enter key. The computer screen flashed and displayed a list of what Lance had to assume were travel routes. The man studied it for a very long time, and while he was doing so, Lance turned back to the seating area and found the woman who'd been waiting was gone. She'd slipped out while their backs had been turned.

Calm down, Lance. It was probably just time for her bus to board. Or maybe she went to the restroom.

"To be honest," the man behind the ticket window started, bringing Lance's attention back, "I can get her there on one of the two busses waiting—the one that leaves in"—he checked his watch—"a half hour. But the quickest route—only one transfer—would be to leave from the Ocean City station. That way she'd be there"—he leaned close to the screen and played *Where's Waldo* again—"early evening, probably before supper."

Lance thought about the woman who had been there and now wasn't, the way her eyes had lingered on them. Thought about a thirty-minute wait, essentially turning Diana into a sitting duck. He looked at Todd. "Can you drive her to Ocean City? Right now?"

And Lance gave Todd credit on another count. The guy didn't even hesitate. "Yes. I've got a bud down there." He shrugged. "Seems like a good time for a day trip. I'll call in sick to the diner."

Lance nodded. Asked the guy behind the window if he had a piece of paper and something to write with, which the man pushed through the little slot in the glass. Lance took it and scribbled two things on the sheet, tore it free and passed the pad and pen back to the man.

He turned and held the paper up to Diana, pointing to the first word he'd written. "Hillston. It's a town in Virginia. I want you to go there. I have a friend there who will help you. He's helped me my entire life, and I promise you can trust him." He pointed to the second thing he'd written. "Marcus Johnston," Lance said. "That's his name. He's the mayor of Hillston. That means he's in charge of everything. Find him, and tell him Lance sent you." Then he folded the piece of paper in half and handed it to Diana.

"You'll make sure she gets on the right bus?" Lance asked Todd. "Help her get a ticket?"

Todd nodded. "Of course. Hillston, Virginia. Got it."

Lance found an ATM near the entrance to the alcove where the restrooms were and got enough cash to get Diana a bus ticket and some food. He pulled the bills free from the machine and turned to go back to—

Jerry the janitor was standing at the far end of the bus station, next to a row of vending machines that were lined up along the rear wall by a push-bar door with a dimly lit EXIT sign glowing above it. He was leaning against the wall, wearing the same outfit Lance had seen him wearing before when they'd encountered each other in the bathroom, and his hands were stuffed into his pockets. Casual. Looking like he hadn't a care in the world.

He was staring straight at Lance.

No question about it.

Lance stared back, feeling the fumes of rage begin to boil and spark inside him. He breathed in deeply, trying to calm himself.

What can you do? he wondered. *What can you actually do about it that the police can't? Just make the call once you're away from here.*

But the way Jerry was staring at him angered Lance. It was almost as if the janitor knew that Lance knew what he really was, and he was taunting him. It was more a feeling than a look, actually. Something permeating the air and toying with Lance. Clawing at him.

He turned around and returned to his two companions. He handed Diana the money, pushing it into her hand along with the note. "Go on," he said. "Find Marcus Johnston. He'll be expecting you."

"You sure you don't want to come with us?" Todd asked. "You can catch a bus there just like she's going to. I mean, if you need to get out of here, might as well, right?"

Until the trip to the ATM, Lance had not fully convinced himself of a decision one way or the other. Stay or go?

He looked over his shoulder and saw Jerry in the same spot, standing completely still, his eyes focused wholly on Lance. And then the man gave a small nod, so subtle it was barely noticeable. And then he winked. And then he turned and pushed down on the door's bar and swung it open just wide enough to slip outside.

Lance turned back to Todd. "No. I'll figure something else out. Just get her out of here, okay?"

Todd nodded.

Lance held out his hand, and Todd shook it. "Thank you for your help, Todd. Seriously. You're probably saving her life, or at least allowing her to actually have one."

Then Lance said his goodbye to Diana, giving her a hug which she returned timidly, but with eyes that said she was grateful. He wished her luck and told her everything would work out. It was a statement he had to force himself to believe. He had faith in Marcus Johnston, but he didn't know how much faith he had in the United States immigration office.

Todd and Diana turned and left the bus station.

Lance adjusted the straps of his backpack, turned around, and headed for the rear door. Off to find Jerry the janitor and tell him to never wink at him again.

His mother used to tell him he had to pick his battles.

Lance was picking this one.

[28]

By the time Lance had made his way to the rear exit of the bus station's lobby and was reaching out to grip the door's push bar and throw it down and step out into the early-morning darkness, he'd managed to come up with several scenarios that could play out. The most desirable of these scenarios would be a civilized and articulate chat between him and Jerry the janitor, one in which, at the end of it all, Lance would help the man to see the error in his ways and Jerry would march himself right down to the police station and turn himself in.

The least desirable, yet unfortunately more likely, was Jerry the janitor waiting just outside the bus station's door with some sort of large blunt object gripped in his hands—maybe a metal pipe, or a baseball bat full of protruding nails—that would render Lance unconscious if not dead with one or two precise blows to the skull.

There were scenarios in between these two extremes, of course, but all Lance could seem to focus on was the image of himself lying facedown on the asphalt with nail holes in his head.

Which was why, when he did grip the door's push bar and

ease it down, slowly inching the door open bit by bit and peering out, his mind completely froze.

He was convinced he was seeing himself, just as he'd imagined it, except he was on his back on the asphalt, just beside a large dumpster, his nightmare come true. He was so distracted by this impossible reality that he pushed the door open the rest of the way and stepped outside, letting the door slam closed behind him.

He found himself standing in a large alley between the bus station and what appeared to be some sort of small warehouse on the opposite side of the open space. Empty, dark, quiet. A lone overhead light mounted above the bus station's door cast an ugly yellow tint in a circle of light several feet around him. The body, which he'd at first thought to be himself—though he knew that couldn't be, not really—was half in this circle of light, and half-hidden in the shadow of the Dumpster. Lance took two steps forward and stopped. Closer now, he recognized the boots, noticed the blue work pants. His heart sped up, his mind chased it. More confused now than ever, Lance hurried his way the last few feet to the body, stepping around it and coming up to the side, crouching down to see the face in the darkness.

It was Jerry the janitor.

Lance could see no visible wounds and no signs of external distress, but it was clear the man was dead. He wasn't breathing, and Lance was certain that if he were to risk feeling for a pulse, he wouldn't find one. The man had one eye open and the other closed, the white of the opened one bloodshot and dark. His mouth was frozen in a half-open scream.

But ... how? He was alive less than a minute ago.

And as if his confusion were not crippling enough at that point, when a shadow shifted in Lance's peripheral vision, and he quickly stood and looked to the right of the dumpster, he officially thought he'd lost his mind when a shape emerged from the darkness and stepped closer toward the circle of light.

It was Jerry the janitor. Upright. Moving. *Alive.*

Lance stepped back but found himself unable to turn around completely and run away. He forced himself to stay put, his head bouncing up and down, back and forth between the dead Jerry on the ground and the alive Jerry walking toward him.

Twins? Lance thought. *Are they twins?*

It was the only rational thought he could muster. The only logical thing that would allow Lance's mind to accept what he was seeing.

Or it's a fake, he tried. *A dummy, a decoy. Like a movie prop.*

The Jerry the janitor that was alive and moving was taking slow steps toward Lance now, and Lance began to match the man step for step, only moving backward, keeping his distance. He searched the man's face for some sort of explanation, waited for a him to say something.

The man said nothing.

But he didn't have to.

And that was when Lance felt it, the grim grip of what he suddenly knew could be the only other explanation. Something that he wouldn't have been prepared for—not fully—if he hadn't already seen it. Once before. Back in Hillston. The night everything had changed.

Lance took one last step backward and then felt himself bump against something low and solid behind him. He stumbled, caught his balance, and then turned around to find a car parked in the alley. He'd not seen it when he'd come through the bus station's door, as he'd been too distracted by the body by the dumpster. It was a boxy midsize SUV. In the dark it looked green in color, or maybe blue. Maybe a mix of both. Honda emblem on the front. The front passenger door opened, and a tall, lean figure got out.

Lance felt his entire body go cold with fear, his blood turning to ice water. His heart felt as if somebody had cranked the dial from one to a hundred.

The tall figure took one step closer, its features now just visible in the glow of the light.

"Hello, Lance," the Reverend said.

Lance turned his head, slowly, looking over his shoulder.

Instead of Jerry the janitor, the Surfer stood silently, his arms crossed and his long hair twitching in the breeze.

Lance stayed still, his head half-turned over his shoulder, allowing himself to keep both the Reverend and the Surfer in his peripheral vision. But he looked at neither of them, not really. His eyes looked straight, his mind so flooded with emotion at the sight of them—the two who he'd been trying so hard to avoid, the last people on earth he'd ever wanted to see again, yet also the two people that he'd vowed to himself he'd make them pay for what they'd done if he ever did see them again—that his body was locked in a state of indecision. Run or fight?

Could he ever get revenge for what they'd done? Could he ever bring his mother back?

The answer was no.

Did he understand enough about what these two really were to have a chance at besting them?

Another no, he regretted to admit.

And Lance had to keep going. Sugar Beach wasn't his last stop on this journey he'd been forced into. He knew it wasn't enough, what he'd accomplished so far. Nowhere near enough to feel as though he'd honored his mother's sacrifice. And honestly, would anything he'd do ever be enough?

Another no. But he knew, deep down, he was meant for more.

And there was someone else, too.

(*"Play smart, okay?"*)

There was no way he was going to let the last conversation he'd had with Leah be the final one. No, another part of him—a new part that was only a seedling and steadily starting to grow—had come to realize that the two of them might just be getting started, and he was so eager to see what they would become.

The Reverend, patient and collected, spoke: "Let's go for a ride, Lance. I think you'll be interested to hear what I have to say."

And that was when the Surfer, who'd somehow managed to silently close the gap between himself and Lance in a half-blink of an eye, wrapped his tanned and weathered arms around Lance in a bear hug, and Lance felt as though he were suddenly falling down a deep, dark well, his energy draining as the ground rushed toward him.

He's so cold, was the last thought Lance had before there was nothing.

———

But the nothing did not last long. Lance came to a moment later, seated in the backseat of the Honda with his seat belt securely fastened. The Reverend sat in front of him, the Surfer driving slowly toward the mouth of the alley and making a left to return to the front of the bus station and the road beyond.

In his semi-groggy state, as if he'd just woken from a long nap or come out from under anesthesia, Lance could only muster one thought: *I've lost.*

As they rounded the corner and drove by the front of the bus station, Lance caught a glimpse of a woman leaning against the wall near the entrance, emblazoned by the neon signage. She was smoking a cigarette and talking on her cell phone.

It was the woman from earlier who'd been waiting inside the bus station. The one Lance thought had let her eyes linger too long on his party.

She was staring now, too, as the vehicle drove by, and her eyes seemed to seek Lance out in the backseat.

She started talking faster into her phone.

The Surfer pulled out onto the main road and started heading back toward the heart of Sugar Beach, toward the diner and Sand Dollar Road. Back the way Lance had just run from.

[29]

THE EFFECTS OF THE SURFER'S GRIP ON LANCE—*WHAT DID he do to me?*—had almost completely worn off by the time the bus station's neon signage had faded away in the Honda's rearview. With his head feeling less full of cotton, Lance sat up straighter in the seat, something bulky digging into his back. He looked down and saw the straps of his backpack over his shoulders. When he'd blacked out as the Surfer had grabbed him from behind, they must have put him into the vehicle as quickly as possible, not even bothering to remove his bag before they'd tossed him into the seat. They had managed to throw the seat belt across his torso and buckle it. Safety first, apparently, even during an abduction.

He shifted in the seat, trying to adjust the bag so it was no longer poking into his kidneys. He looked down to his hands and feet, found them free. The Reverend and the Surfer hadn't taken the time to bind him, or make any effort to keep him from running away from them. Lance looked out the window at the passing expanse of land and then up at the car's speedometer. Even at their current speed of forty-five miles per hour, risking jumping out of a moving vehicle would likely be a recipe for broken bones and sprained joints and surly a few deep scrapes and gashes. The Reverend and the Surfer would simply stop the car and reload him into the back like a bag of garbage that had fallen off a truck on the way to the dump.

He could try attacking them. Reach up and wrap his hands around the Reverend's throat and squeeze until the man's eyes popped free from their sockets. But the Surfer...

Lance remembered that awful moment back in the alley when the man—*he's not a man*—had enveloped Lance in his arms and squeezed with strength that seemed so ... wrong. And the coldness, both physically and the drowning sense of fading away Lance had felt ... it was as if the Surfer possessed inside him the opposite of whatever creates life. He held in his hands whatever destroyed it.

Lance could not fight them both. If he went after the Reverend, the Surfer might simply reach out with one hand and grab Lance's wrist and toss him right back into the blackness.

So Lance's options were ... limited. He tried to stay calm. Had to be patient and wait for an opportunity. Had to have faith that an opportunity would show itself.

And then he remembered the body—Jerry the janitor lying dead in alley. What had they done to him? Why had they—

"I think that somebody with your notion for helping people would not be too upset about the janitor's abrupt end," the Reverend said, only the words were not coming from his mouth, they were coming from inside Lance's head. Lance's stomach dropped and his heart rate spiked for a moment, fear and adrenaline surging again. He'd forgotten. It'd seemed like an eternity since those few days in Hillston where he'd first seen the Reverend and the Surfer, had learned how powerful they were. The Reverend could get inside his head. Lance didn't know to what extent—if the man could actually dig through his memories like a file cabinet, or if he could only monitor Lance's thoughts in real time. Either way, it was disturbing and humiliating.

Ahead, the diner came into view, lights bouncing off its shiny exterior.

"I just want you to know," the Reverend said, aloud this time, "it was never our intention for your mother to lose her life that night."

And his voice cut through the car's silence and sliced at Lance.

"Don't you ever talk to me about my mother," Lance said through gritted teeth. "You killed her. Both of you."

The Reverend sighed and signaled for the Surfer to take the right turn onto Sand Dollar Road once they'd reached the diner, saying, "We'll hit the highway." Then he turned to Lance and said, "The way I recall the events, your mother was the one who jumped in front of our vehicle. Some might say she was responsible for her own death, don't you think?"

Lance said nothing. Swallowed down rage that was hot like a coal in his throat.

"I will give her credit where credit is due," the Reverend said. "She did manage to slow us down. Alas"—he turned around in the front seat and looked at Lance for the first time, holding up his hands in a what-can-you-do gesture—"here we are, together again."

The Reverend turned back around, and Lance found himself balling his hands into fists.

"It's a shame, really," the Reverend said. "She would have gone on without you, you know? She could have continued once you'd moved on. And we were always going to get you, Lance. You must have realized that by now. Always. So in the end ... she just wasted what life she had left to live."

Something wet dripped down onto Lance's shorts, and he

looked down, startled. Another drop followed, and he was even more surprised to find that he'd started to cry, warm tears making their way slowly down his cheeks.

Lance Brody did not cry often. Almost never. He cleared his throat and wiped his face with the back of his hands and steeled himself against what he now recognized as the Reverend playing some sort of psychological game with him. He stayed quiet, collecting his thoughts. Looked out the window and saw the donut shop as they passed by. The outside was dark, but there were a few lights on inside, back in the kitchen. He saw a figure walk by the cash register, thought it might be April.

There was really only one thing Lance was sure of at this point: the Reverend and the Surfer did not seem to want to kill him, or do him any immediate major harm. Otherwise, they'd have done so already. They wanted him for something more. His own abilities, Lance could only assume. For what reason, he did not know. But if they'd chased him this far ... maybe it was more than them simply wanting him.

Maybe they needed him.

This thought alone gave Lance a new boost of energy, a sudden surge in confidence that maybe, just maybe, he might actually be more in control of his own fate here than he'd realized in the beginning.

These two terrified him, each in their own unique way, but at that moment Lance understood that they would not end his life. But he might have to fight to keep it from becoming theirs.

"Is this a sex thing?" Lance asked.

And now it was the Reverend who sat silently for a moment before asking, "What do you mean?"

Lance shrugged, "Oh, maybe it's nothing. I just know that your kind—you know, men of the cloth—sometimes you like fool around with young boys. I know I'm a little older than that, but maybe you don't really mind. Is that what this is all about?"

A stoplight turned red and the Surfer brought the car to a stop, his face stoic and seemingly uncaring about anything happening around him. The Reverend said, "I understand what you're doing. You're attempting to use humor to make yourself feel better, or maybe try to get a rise out of me for reasons that will benefit your situation."

"Sort of like you were doing by talking about my mother?" Lance volleyed back.

The Reverend shook his head. "On the contrary. I was merely stating a fact. Your own emotional connection to your mother impaired your judgment of the situation."

"You talk like a robot."

"I speak truthfully."

"And your friend talks like he's a Teenage Mutant Ninja Turtle."

Nobody seemed to know what to say after this.

The light turned green and the Surfer drove on. They were approaching the expensive rental houses now. Those giant beach sentinels where a few happy families were currently sleeping after a long day of fun in the sun and sand. No idea what Evil was passing by on the street, just outside their windows.

Because despite what little Lance knew about these two, he knew that they were on the opposite side. Lance fought the battle for the good in the world. These two sought to destroy it.

Lance sighed, feigning as though he'd grown quite bored. "You know, you could make this a lot less dramatic if you'd just tell me what it is you want from me. How about we try that and speed this whole thing along?"

Instead of an answer, the Reverend asked a question of his own. "Have you ever wondered if there are others like you, Lance?"

Lance had been ready for a quick retort, something just to

keep the man talking, but the question stopped him in his tracks. Derailed his train of thought. Because of course he had. He'd wondered about this his entire life. Wondered if he were truly as alone as he felt.

"There *are* others, Lance. We've found them. Just like we found you."

Lance said nothing. Was both stunned by this revelation and also torn between accepting it as truth or rejecting it as just another tactic the Reverend was using to try and dupe him into complying.

"You'll join them," the Reverend said. "And with you … together we'll—"

Something big and fast-moving jutted into Lance's peripheral vision, and the Surfer made a noise that sounded like a growl as he stood on the Honda's brakes, causing tires to scream on the asphalt as the vehicle skidded to a stop.

But it wasn't fast enough. They'd slowed enough so that the collision would be minimal, but the impact was still enough for Lance to get thrown forward before his seat belt caught and threw him back against his seat, the fabric digging deeply across his shoulder and chest, his world temporarily bouncing back and forth. The front airbags had deployed, exploding with white puffs into the Reverend and the Surfer's faces, and the two clawed at them frantically.

As things settled, and Lance took inventory of himself and found that he was unhurt, there was a tap-tap-tap on the driver's-side window. All three of them looked toward the noise. Outside, standing on the street with a gun pointed directly at the Surfer's head, was one of the largest men Lance had ever seen. The man motioned with the gun for the Surfer to step out of the vehicle.

Lance looked through the windshield and wasn't completely surprised at what he saw.

The black Ford Excursion.
Somebody else had found him.

THEM
(IV)

The tap-tap-tap came again on the window, this time with more authority, the barrel of the sleek handgun echoing loudly in the Element's cabin.

"Out. Now!" The man waving the gun had a voice like he could get the part of Darth Vader the next time they made a *Star Wars* sequel. It was impactful. Punched you in the gut. The Surfer turned his head slowly and looked at the Reverend, awaiting instructions. The Reverend looked over the deflated airbags, through the windshield and across the crumpled hood. A large black SUV was in the middle of the road, perpendicular to them. Blocking their way. It was what they'd crashed into. He looked again at the crumpled hood, a steady stream of steam puffing from one of the panel gaps, then he turned in his seat and looked back to Lance—their captive. Though the Reverend didn't like that word. *If the boy only knew what we could do together...*

They were going to need a new vehicle. And the black SUV, despite a dented passenger door, looked like it would be more than adequate. It was just a shame it wasn't a different color. The Surfer would have liked that.

The Reverend nodded once to his partner, saying, "I'll handle it. Be ready if this man decides he won't allow for amicable conversation. But"—the Reverend looked at the enormous man outside the driver's window— "I don't think we'll have any problem here."

The Surfer shrugged, as if the decision meant nothing to him. Then he pushed open the door and began to step out.

"Easy, damn it! Easy. Hands away from your body. That's it," the man with the gun said. When the Surfer was fully out of the car, the man leaned down and peered into the cabin. "You, too, old man." He waved the gun toward Lance. "And bring that son-of-bitch with you. Now, damn it!"

The Reverend did not turn around when he spoke to the boy, but as he opened the door and began to get out, he said, "Stay where you are, Lance. Don't make this worse with a futile attempt to escape. This will be over soon." Then, right before he closed the door: "You can see your mother again, you know that, right? We can show you how."

The look on the boy's face told the Reverend all he needed to know. He'd baited the hook, and the boy had bitten. The mother was proving to be useful, even after her death.

He slammed the door closed and stood straight, holding his hands in the air innocently.

"Over here," the man with gun said. "And bring the fucking boy, like I asked."

The man holding the gun had to be at least six nine, maybe six ten, and was built like he swallowed football linemen for breakfast before he went to the gym. He wore mesh athletic shorts and a long-sleeved t-shirt that looked painted on as it strained against all his mountainous muscles. His sneakers looked like they could safely evacuate small dogs in the event of a hurricane. There was a large bandage above the man's left temple, spotted with blood seeping through, and the Reverend wondered if the man had run into a door frame, forgetting to duck.

The Reverend could not dispute the fact that the man was a giant, capable of great feats of physical strength and dominance.

But he had a tiny brain. One which the Reverend had already begun to probe inside of without the man ever knowing. Getting inside the head of somebody like Lance was harder, required more effort to get around the defenses. Lance's mind was close in strength to what this man before him was in physical strength. Getting inside the head of the man with the gun was as easy for the Reverend as walking through an open door.

"The boy is very tired," the Reverend said, walking around the rear of the Honda and moving to stand next to the Surfer, who was now leaning casually against the side of the vehicle, his arms crossed, looking bored. "I think he'll stay where he is. He needs to rest."

The giant with the gun looked incredulous, clearly unfamiliar with somebody disobeying his requests. He was an enforcer, that much was certain. "The *hell* did you just say?" He took two steps forward and aimed the gun directly at the Reverend's forehead. Then he reversed his grip, holding the pistol by the barrel and thumping the butt of the weapon against his catcher's mitt of a palm. "Get the boy out now, or I will break your nose. Then, as you're choking on blood, you can tell me how tired he is."

The Surfer slid over, just the tiniest bit closer to the Reverend. The man with the gun didn't even notice, clearly not intimated by either of them. His muscles made him arrogant, and his brain didn't allow him to see this.

The Reverend sighed. He had to hurry this up. Sugar Beach might be small, but eventually somebody would notice this accident. Police would be called. Trouble would be made.

"Magnus, you don't need to be doing this. Whatever this boy has done, it's not worth you getting involved with us right now, okay? Have you ever heard the phrase 'forgive and forget?'"

The giant—the man's whose name was Magnus—opened his mouth to say something that was most likely going to contain expletives and more threats of broken bones, but then stopped, his brain slowly firing synapses and realizing what had just happened.

His wall of a forehead crinkled in confusion, and he stuttered, "How do you know my name?"

"I know a lot about you, Magnus," the Reverend said.

Because he did.

In the few moments it had taken Magnus to walk forward and threaten the Reverend with the butt of his gun, the Reverend had explored every crevice of the man's mind—something else that was much harder to do with Lance. He'd barely been able to penetrate the surface with the boy, which was both incredibly frustrating and also wonderfully exciting.

Such power he has.

But Magnus's mind was like an open book.

The Reverend was able to search until he found why exactly Magnus had decided to stop them, why he was so interested in Lance. Turns out, in typical fashion, the boy had helped a young woman escape from this man's employers, which they felt was an expensive loss of property, one which they clearly meant to gain reparations for. Preferably by recovering their asset, but they'd also accept making sure the individual responsible for their loss was informed he'd made a grievous error. If he happened to divulge the whereabouts of their lost property in the process of such reparations, that would be an added bonus.

There's always a girl, the Reverend thought. *How predictable.*

But on top of all that, as it turned out, Magnus was the reason this girl had been able to get away in the first place. The Reverend explored one of the man's recent memories: Magnus and this girl—a young, pretty blond thing—pressed close together against the wall of a garage, kissing passionately. The same black Expedition that had driven into the road, blocking their path, was parked in the garage, engine still warm as the girl reached down and began massaging between Magnus's legs. And then, as the giant was slipping deeper into his oblivion of sexual stupor, the girl moved quickly, deftly swooping down and grabbing a small portable fire extinguisher that had been sitting in the corner. She'd gripped it in both hands and swung up and across with all her might, and there was a wet *thud* as it connected with Magnus's head. The man dropped limply to the ground with a slurred grunt, and then the girl was running. Out the garage door and into the night.

Magnus seemed to consider the Reverend's statement for a moment ("I know a lot about you, Magnus") and then his eyes shifted and his features hardened again. "You don't know shit 'bout me, old man. Now get him out of the fucking car before I make you. This is your last chance. It's not you I want. It's him."

The Surfer shifted again, closing the gap between himself and the Reverend a tiny bit more.

"The boy is coming with us," the Reverend said.

Magnus stepped forward, raised the butt of the pistol in the air, pulling back for a swing.

"The boy is coming with us," the Reverend said again, only this time, he was in. He'd found the controls and had hooked himself up. He pumped the thoughts into Magnus's consciousness with ease, like pumping gasoline into a car. He flooded Magnus's mind's tank with instructions, interspersing them with memories of things the man had thought nobody else would ever know. The things he made some of the other girls— some of the other *assets*—do, threatening them aimlessly, their fear driving them to perform what he'd requested. The Reverend pushed deeper and—

A noise. Behind him. The boy.

His mental grip on Magnus hadn't slipped much, but it'd been enough for the man to snap somewhat out of the fugue state he'd fallen into at the Reverend's doing, enough for his anger to surface, his humiliation and feeling of violation to push through the barrier the Reverend had started to construct. His eyes lit with rage. He reached out with one hand and wrapped it around the Reverend's throat, slamming the man back against the Element's side, the car rocking with the impact. The Reverend looked to the Surfer out of the corner of his eye, waiting for this partner to spring into action.

But what he saw was the Surfer standing still, facing the opposite direction and looking across the Element's roof, his eyes tracking something.

The Reverend feared he knew what it was, but he had more pressing issues at the moment. He closed his eyes as Magnus squeezed his windpipe, and jumped back in, focusing.

Then he found what he was looking for—an old rugby injury, many years ago before Magnus had ever come to work for his current employers. Something with the left knee. Something that had never quite healed correctly. The Reverend took this thought and cast his eyes to the Surfer, hissing out a strangled, "*Knee!*"

The Surfer moved at once, reaching out and touching the tip of his index finger to Magnus's knee.

And Magnus's grip on the Reverend's throat was all at once gone as he screamed in agony and crumpled to the ground, writhing on the asphalt.

The Reverend spun around and checked inside the Honda, knowing what he'd see.

The boy was gone.

"He, like, totally ran that way," the Surfer said, pointing toward the beach. On the ground behind them, Magnus was still screaming and rolling and ... was he crying? But the Reverend ignored him for a moment, feeling something else in the air, something other than the boy. There were others. Many of them. And they were ... calling for him?

The Reverend turned and looked at Magnus. He could have

made it easier on the man, but Magnus had made him angry. The Reverend said to the Surfer, "End him. And then let's go."

When it was over, the two of them walked across the street and over the dunes, leaving the wrecked cars and Magnus's body in the road. It was sloppy, but the Reverend pressed on.

He could feel it. *It's going to end tonight*, he thought.

Tonight.

LANCE BRODY RAN.

The Reverend's words about being able to see Lance's mother again had knocked Lance back, but only for a moment. Lance was no fool. The Revered had still been playing games, using Lance and his mother's relationship as a basis for deceit and manipulation. He'd even told Lance as much just moments earlier ("Your own emotional connection to your mother impaired your judgment of the situation"), before the black Ford Excursion had stopped their path and the enormous man with the gun had ushered the Reverend and the Surfer out of the car and given Lance the only chance he'd get.

And Lance had taken it.

He knew it posed a risk—as most of Lance's decisions did—because he remembered the image of the lifeless Jerry the janitor lying in the alley. He'd appeared completely unharmed, yet...

The Surfer had powers Lance did not understand. More than he'd thought in the beginning. He was extremely danger-ous. Yet Lance picked up on an odd sort of chain of command between his two assailants. The Surfer, despite his power, seemed only to take orders from the Reverend—unwilling to act completely on his own.

And now Lance was running. He'd waited until it seemed like the three men outside the Honda had been too preoccupied with their situation to notice him—hoping the Reverend truly believed that his promise about Lance's mother would be enough to get Lance to stay put—and then he'd bolted from the car and run straight across the street and over the curb and through the ugly mix of grass and sand and over the dunes and onto the beach.

Toward them.

As Lance had sat in the back of the car, contemplating his options, he'd noticed the flicker of orange and yellow glow in the sky up ahead. The bonfire. The kids on the beach. *Closer than it should be,* he thought. But then he remembered his first night in Sugar Beach, the way the fire had seemed closer then, too. The way he'd felt all at once compelled to head straight toward it.

He felt that now. An urging, a *pull.* He didn't know why, but he needed to get there, at all cost.

So he ran. Not knowing how much time he had. Not knowing if the Reverend and Surfer would chase him, not knowing how fast they were—the Surfer, in particular.

Not knowing if the police would come.

Not knowing if they would see his side of things.

Not knowing if they would believe him.

Which made him think of Marcus Johnston. Which made him think of Diana. Hopefully well on her way to Ocean City, and then on to the help she deserved.

Diana. Lance was hit with the realization that if he'd not chosen to help the girl, he might not have gotten away from the Reverend and the Surfer. The people from the house with the cameras had clearly been looking for Diana, and Lance—whether by speculation or by information given from informants, *spies*, around town who might have been more than willing to say they'd seen Lance talking to the girls. The woman at the bus station had been one of them, Lance knew that for certain now. Which a good place to put a spy if you suspected somebody was trying to get out of town. He remembered the way her eyes had lingered, the image of her talking rapidly on the phone outside the station's lobby as the Honda had driven by. She'd been calling it in. Telling them what to look for. And they'd found him.

And they'd freed him.

Lance had been convinced that the multiple suicides, Loraine Linklatter and the Boundary House, and the girls with their coolers had not been related. And on the surface, they were not. But in Lance's world, through his actions, they'd managed to weave together and set off a chain of events that had brought him here. He'd saved one girl—hopefully an action that would save the others—and now hopefully it'd allowed him to save himself.

The Universe had a plan. Lance just wished it'd let him in on it every now and then.

His lungs began to burn and his nostrils flared against the harsh salty air. His feet grew heavy in the sand, his backpack bouncing up and down with each steady step. He dared not stop to look over his shoulder, afraid of seeing the Surfer, impossibly close and reaching out for him.

And then Lance did stop.

The bonfire was suddenly right before him, just a few yards away.

The spirits of Sugar Beach's five young suicide victims stood in a straight line, like a wall of soldiers waiting for the attack.

They looked at him, all of them, and there was something different in their faces, their eyes. Where before, there had seemed to be an emptiness, a sense of being lost—which, Lance had to figure, they very well might have been—there now seemed to be a sense of understanding. Their features were set in determined purpose. They looked ... prepared. Ready to accomplish their task.

"Behind us," the girl with the red hair said, and then her eyes looked past him and locked onto something else. Lance turned slowly in the sand and looked up the beach. Saw the two unmistakable silhouettes moving toward him. Slowly. Patiently. The moonlight seemed not to reflect from them, but simply be absorbed by them, their images black as a starless night sky.

Until they were closer, and the Reverend and Surfer's features were brought into existence by the glow of the bonfire.

Lance looked back to the redheaded girl and she nodded once. Lance did not argue, did not question. He moved quickly through the sand and around the wall of ghosts and stood a few feet behind them, just past one of the large pieces of driftwood, the heat of the fire burning at his back. Wood cracking and popping as the flames fed.

The Surfer stopped first, maybe fifteen feet from the kids. The Reverend noticed and abruptly stopped as well, looking to his partner for an explanation. The Surfer turned his head and spoke softly, impossible for Lance to hear as the waves crashed and the wind carried the sound away. The Reverend's eyes glanced back to Lance, then seemed to search the space around him. The Surfer said something else and the Reverend nodded and stood straight, speaking loudly. "Your friends can't help you, Lance. They aren't of this world."

Lance did not attempt to dispute this.

But he noticed that despite the Reverend's words, the man was not coming any closer.

Lance replayed the last few moments in his head, the way the Surfer had stopped first, the way the Reverend's eyes had searched the sand and landed on nothing but Lance. *He can't see them*, Lance thought. *The Surfer can, but* he *can't.*

It was useful information to have—a stronger idea of what each of these two was capable of. But Lance couldn't help but feel that, depending on how the next few minutes went, it might never matter.

"My partner is stronger than them, Lance. Truly." Then, "You've only seen a sample of what he can do. *I've* only seen a sample, myself."

But they weren't moving. Both stood still in the sand, their faces bathed in orange. The Surfer's eyes were dancing along the line of spirits, calculating, as if trying to form an attack, weighing the odds.

And that was when it happened. The redheaded girl, who was on the end of the line to Lance's right, reached her left hand out and grabbed the hand of the boy next to her, the one in the sweatshirt and jeans.

And Lance would swear the sky darkened.

The boy reached his hand out and grabbed the hand of the boy to his left, the one with the backward baseball cap.

And Lance would swear the noise from the water grew quieter.

"*Lance*," the Reverend said, his voice growing with anger ... or was it fear? "Don't make me send him to get you. It will not end well. We can make this easy. We can work together. Don't you want to see the others? Don't you want to be with your same kind?"

The second boy reached his hand and clasped the hand of the boy to his left.

And Lance would swear the flames behind him roared and stretched and doubled in size.

There was only one link to the chain left. The older girl, the one Lance had to assume was the first, the one with the master's degree in biology who had been well on her way to a PhD, was on the left end of the line, the two girls bookending the boys. She stood tall and straight and defiant, as if ready for the challenge.

The air began to hum and fill with static. All the hair on Lance's body stood at attention. His teeth buzzed, seemed to pulse with the wave of energy that began to blanket them. Something that might have been lightning flashed, but it was too close, not in the sky but almost directly above their heads. Lance flinched, jumping back, but the kids stood their ground, hands linked.

"Go!" the Reverend yelled, and the Surfer charged the line, a burst of speed that seemed to flash across the distance in a nearly imperceivable moment of time. So fast that Lance did not even understand it had happened.

And at the same time, the girl on the end, who might one day have been one of the world's greatest scientists, who'd had such potential and had tragically decided that help was something she could never receive, grabbed the hand of the boy next to her, completing the chain.

There was a great clap of thunder—thunder that was too close—and this time Lance screamed in surprise. The fire behind him erupted to the sky like it'd been doused with a barrel of lighter fluid, nearly knocking Lance to his knees.

The Surfer charged full speed toward the wall of spirits, and just as Lance had the terrible thought—*he's going to go right through them!*—because the Reverend was right, they were not of this world, the kids absorbed the impact, their line warping and giving slightly under the momentum, and then they bounced back like a rubber band snapping back into place. The

238

Surfer was flung backward with a grunt that sounded more surprised than angry.

"Again!" the Reverend yelled, this time taking a step forward himself, though it was a small one. His eyes were on Lance, and Lance could see the flames flickering in them.

And then the Surfer made his next charge, only this time when the spirits absorbed the blow, halting the Surfer's stride, the air around them came alive—a fresh wave of energy rushing across the beach, landing on top of them. Wind did not so much blow as it did scream, like it was being pulled away, painfully, against its will.

Lance's head buzzed so loudly he fell to the sand and covered his ears with his hands, squeezed his eyes shut just long enough to regain his balance. He could feel it pulsing through him, whatever force this was. Felt it stir his stomach and squeeze his heart and compress his lungs.

Then he heard the growl, like some rabid animal caught in a snare. The noise was vicious and frantic and enraged. Lance opened his eyes and saw that the spirits had formed a tight circle around the Surfer, their hands still linked together as they inched their way closer and closer, eating up any empty space around him. The Surfer growled again, a sound that should never come out of a human's mouth, and he struck out with hands and feet, slashing and shoving and punching. The spirits of the dead kids took the blows, occasionally slowed by the attack. But each time one of them looked as if the strike had actually caused some sort of celestial damage, a new rush of wind and energy would thump the beach like the hit of some unseen subwoofer, the fire would surge with tall, fresh flames, and the kids would push forward.

And once the circle had tightened completely, the spirits the noose, the Surfer the neck about to snap, there was an absolute eruption of thunder, so loud that Lance was literally blinded as his head felt turned to jelly from the noise. His vision blackened, then became fuzzy, and then...

When Lance was able to see again, he thought he might have had a stroke, or suffered some other brain injury.

Behind the circle of spirits and the trapped, struggling Surfer, behind the Reverend, who stood and stared as his partner fought invisible forces, frozen with uncertainty and uselessness, the beach and the rest of the world beyond it seemed to be cracked in two, like a picture frame glass that had split, causing the image it covered to be skewed and uneven, two halves of an imperfect image. Puzzle pieces that did not line up.

And the crack between the two halves widened, the wind screaming now as if a hurricane was being born right there before them all. Lance felt as though he were being lifted from the ground, floating across the sand toward the crack.

And then it was a gap, the two halves of the beach seeming to be pulled apart like curtains on a theater stage, ready to reveal the show. Only there was no show—when the two sides of the beach pulled apart, there was...

Nothing.

The only word Lance's mind could find was *black*. But this was more than that, and also less. It was as if the world had decided not to fill this part in. It was simply ... empty. It didn't exist.

But it did.

Because Lance was seeing it.

And Lance was not seeing it.

It hurt to think about.

But then the spirits moved forward again, wrangling the Surfer, who was now snarling and growling and clearly understanding what was about to happen.

And Lance understood too. He began to move forward,

propelled by the wind that now seemed to be being sucked into the emptiness between the picture pieces, as if by a giant vacuum. He headed for the Reverend, who was now standing with wide eyes and an open mouth, staring at the nothingness that had opened behind him. The Reverend's eyes darted from the blackness and then back to his partner, who Lance thought must look to the Reverend as if he was walking very awkwardly toward this new hole in the universe. Then, just as the spirits reached the point where, with another two steps, they would have begun to disappear into the gap, falling into whatever lay beyond and taking the Surfer with them, the Reverend moved. Whether out of genuine compassion for his partner or because he knew that if the spirits of the young kids succeeded in tossing the Surfer into this unknown space, the mission would be over and everything lost, the Reverend took off across the ground and positioned himself in between the Surfer and the blackness. He dug his heels in and held up his hands, ready to push. The wind whipped at his shirt and pants, plastering them against him. His hair pulled back from his head and revealed a bone-white scalp.

The group of spirits and the Surfer hit the Reverend's hands, and the man dug in further and yelled with a grunt of strength and desperation. The group slowed as they collided with him, and with this small moment of resistance, the Surfer seemed to find a second wind, a new surge of energy. He roared with frustration and managed to get a kick into the gut of the redheaded girl, causing her to lose her grip on the hand of the boy next to her. Which was enough of a weakening for the Surfer to push forward, assisted by the Reverend, and begin to slowly move the entire circle backward, away from the blackness.

He's stronger than them, Lance remembered the Reverend's words. And maybe the Reverend had been right.

No, Lance thought. And then he actually yelled it,

surprising himself, screaming the word as he ran full speed toward the pile of ghosts and the Reverend and the thing called the Surfer that wasn't really a man at all, and threw himself into the pile, lowering his shoulder and aiming for the Surfer.

And before he made impact, as he passed through the spirits of the kids who'd ended their own lives, he was flooded with memories and emotions and parts of each of them. Birthdays and holidays. Nervousness and elation. First kisses and last dances. Excitement and fear. Family and friends. Joy and sadness. Hobbies and skills. Music. Laughter. Worry. Smiles. Doubt. Tears. He lived all their lives in a span of half a second, and he wished he could go back to each of them, wanted to hug them and be their friend and...

And there was nothing.

Then there was just the end.

And Lance's shoulder slammed into the Surfer's chest and he let out a growl of his own and used his long legs to dig in and push and he heard the Reverend scream something he could not make out over the howling of the wind and buzz of the energy and then they were falling, all of them, over the edge of the cracked picture fame and into the nothing. First the Reverend was gone, sucked into the void with a scream that was sliced in half, silenced, and then the Surfer followed, tangled in a knot of limbs from the spirits of the kids. One by the one they were vanishing into the void, momentum carrying them all forward and beyond.

And that was when Lance realized he was going to fall in with them, and fear unlike any he'd ever known erased all thoughts from his mind except a strong, unflinching, undeniable will to live. There was that thought, and then there was also a name: *Leah.*

Something shoved him back, as if invisible hands had reached out and thumped him in the chest, knocking him the opposite direction with unnatural strength. He felt himself flailing through the air, pushing against the wind, and then he landed hard on his back, his head smashing back against the earth.

And then it was over.

[31]

WHEN HE OPENED HIS EYES, HE STARED STRAIGHT INTO THE blackness and thought for one fleeting second that he'd actually fallen in, had joined the rest of them in that other place, the gap in the universe.

But then his vision cleared and he saw the pale light of the emerging dawn. Felt his lungs fill with air and the scent of salt-water and sand and everything living. He sat up, slowly, his world speckled with black fuzzies for a moment before his head cleared and his equilibrium settled, and he was able to stand, brushing sand from his hands.

Everything was back to normal. He looked up the beach and saw one straight image, the two halves of the picture pushed back together as they should be, not even the hint of a seam. The howling wind had been replaced by only a gentle breeze, carrying sea mist and grains of sand along with it. The buzzing in his head was gone, replaced by a dull headache which was the result of his fall.

They'd saved him.

Once Lance had figured out who the young spirits by the fire had actually been—thanks in part to Leah, verifying the number of suicide deaths during one of her phone calls—he'd been under the impression his job was to help them. Another task on the list which he did not understand. Turned out, they'd been waiting to save *him*—even if they hadn't known this until the time had arrived.

But maybe we saved each other, Lance thought. Maybe, in their protection against the Surfer, and their tumble into the blackness, they'd not only allowed Lance to stay alive and free but also squared themselves with the Universe. Maybe when they'd passed out of this world and into whatever lay beyond, they'd crossed into a place where they could be truly happy— maybe for the first time ever. And now, for eternity.

Lance wanted to believe that. Wondered if maybe wherever those kids had ended up, his mother was there, too. He hoped she would bake them a pie.

"There's one more thing now," a girl's voice said from behind him. Lance spun, completely jarred from his thoughts, and found the spirit of the older girl, the first victim who'd been standing so alone down by the water when he'd first seen her, sitting on one of the pieces of driftwood. The fire had burned away to almost nothing now, and there was only a dim glow to light her against the faded background of the beach as the first light of the sun turned the world from black to gray.

"What?" Lance asked.

"I'll take her home," the girl said. "She'll never get there alone."

And Lance remembered.

The girl was right. There was one more thing.

———

When he crossed the street, after passing through the little park where Loraine Linklatter had done yoga for the last time, he looked up the road and saw tiny specks surrounded by flashing emergency lights and people scurrying about. The scene of the accident, where the Excursion had been step one in stopping the Reverend and the Surfer, where there was probably a dead body and lots of unanswerable questions.

Lance knew he needed to be gone before anybody could find a reason to track him down and question what he knew. He laughed at this thought. Because really, in the end, what did he know? Only that it was time to move on.

There were no police cars or ambulances or anything at all outside the Boundary House, and based on the lack of any barrier or bright yellow crime scene tape discouraging entry, Lance could only assume that no report of gunfire had been called in when Loraine Linklatter had shot herself. Maybe he should be the one to call it in. Maybe not. He didn't see how it mattered at this point. Somebody would find Loraine Linklatter eventually, and Lance wanted to be as far away from Sugar Beach as possible when that happened.

He found her body exactly where he'd left it, slumped over the kitchen table. Only now, she looked different. Less real than before, as death took its toll. Lance stood in the kitchen doorway, silent and waiting.

Daisy was sitting in the breakfast nook in the seat opposite her mother's body. Her tiny feet were crossed, her legs swinging back and forth. She looked ... impatient.

"Daisy?" Lance said, stepping closer.

She turned to look at him, and Lance could see her face was full of something like frustration crossed with anger. "Where is she?" Daisy said. "She should be here by now, right?"

Lance instantly understood and felt a piece of his heart break. "Daisy, I don't think she's coming." He paused, tried to think how to explain. "Not everyone ... not all people who pass away stay here. I think you know that, right?"

Daisy was still for a moment and then nodded, once, twice, before her face fell and she cried out, "But she's my mommy and she's supposed to be with me! Why am I here and she's not? We were supposed to be together again now!"

Daisy leaned forward and reached out and Lance watched as her hand passed through her mother's head as she meant to stroke the woman's hair. And it was then that Lance wondered if Daisy knew the truth, deep down. If, in reality, she knew that her mother had been the one to officially end her life, end her suffering. He wondered if it mattered.

He decided that it didn't.

"Daisy," he said, "there's somebody else who can help you. She can help you cross on to whatever's next and"—he felt a little guilty at this next part, because he had no way of knowing if it was true—"she'll help you find your mother."

He said these things because Lance guessed that eternity in the other place, with or without her mother at her side, was infinitely better than being trapped in the human world alone.

Daisy looked at him with scrutinizing eyes, as if ready to call his bluff. But then, after what felt like a very long time, she took one last look at her mother's body, then around the kitchen, the way one does when one sells a house and is making their final departure before heading off to what's next, reveling in memories and history.

She moved from the table and followed Lance to the front door, where she paused for just a second, either unsure she wanted to go through with it, or uncertain she actually possessed the ability to cross the threshold.

Lance figured she did. Now, she did.

Daisy took a step, then another.

Lance said goodbye to both of them—Daisy, and the spirit of the girl who'd been waiting patiently on the piece of driftwood. Thanked them both for everything. Then he stood by the burned-out remains of the bonfire as the girl took Daisy's hand and led her down to the water, where they both walked slowly into the surf, fading away into nothing as the sun crept over the horizon.

Lance thought it might be the most beautiful thing he'd ever seen.

HER
(IV)

Leah drove her mother's ancient VW Beetle down the driveway of her family's home. The one where her father lived alone now —one wife and one son deceased, one daughter...

One daughter ready to move on.

Leah had made the decision for herself, she knew that. But she also knew that if it wasn't for Lance, this would never have happened. She would have never been able to get the closure she needed—her *father* wouldn't have either, which was maybe the most important part—or the personal strength required to leave this place. Leave Westhaven. Leave the only place she'd ever known.

But Lance had given her that. Some of it directly, and some of it indirectly. He'd been an inspiration to her, more than he probably knew. His bravery, his sense of duty and purpose, his desire to help and do good. Leah wanted to go on this journey with him. There was nothing left for her in Westhaven.

Lance and she were similar in that way—they both had reached a moment in their lives where they'd been presented with a choice between moving forward and chasing the light, or staying put and succumbing to the darkness.

Lance had chosen the light.

And so would she.

She loved him.

Her father had understood. She'd chosen not to focus on Lance being such a large factor in her decision, but instead on the desire to live her life for once. He'd accepted this humbly enough. There'd been tears, though, from both sides of the table. And there'd been big hugs and wet kisses, and as she'd pulled away from him, he'd taken her by the shoulders—a lifetime of memories and hardships and forgiveness passing between them —and he'd said, "Go and live, baby girl. I know wherever you go, that place will be better because of it."

So she drove on, through her hometown and headed toward the highway, no destination in mind. There was only one thing left to do.

She pulled over at a rest stop thirty miles out of town and picked up her phone to make the call.

[32]

LANCE HAD WALKED MAYBE THREE MILES, LEAVING SUGAR
Beach behind him as the sun climbed into the sky in the east.
Sand Dollar Road had eventually become a two-lane highway,
heading north toward the future, and Lance walked along the
shoulder with his mind partially in the clouds.

After watching Daisy cross over with the help of her new
friend, Lance had walked a long way on the beach before eventually making his way back to the road. He knew he needed to
leave, but he didn't want to risk returning to the bus station—
didn't want to stay in Sugar Beach a second longer than he
needed to. There'd been so much loss there, so much sadness.

The sun felt good on his face.

He thought about the fight on the beach, the way the
Reverend and Surfer had fallen into the blackness. And what
surprised Lance the most as he considered this was the lack of
liberation he felt. Those two had been the entire reason his life
had been uprooted. The reason his mother was dead and Lance
sent on this strange journey to nowhere in particular. And now
they were gone and Lance felt ... the same?

Okay, not exactly the same. There was a large part of him

that was relieved, that felt as though he were allowed to breathe for the first time in months. But there was another part of him, a part lurking in the back of his mind in the shadows, that did not believe that the Reverend and the Surfer were truly gone. They'd only been temporarily displaced.

A battle won in a greater war.

But, with them or without them, Lance also understood that his mission was to continue. There would always be another Sugar Beach, another Ripton's Grove, another Westhaven. And many, many places in between.

There was just too much darkness in the world. And Lance Brody carried a torch, helping to relight the way.

Another mile down the highway, he came across a small gas station with old-style pumps and a handwritten sign out front advertising softshell crab sandwiches. The slanting wooden building was the color of dust and looked as though two men should have been sitting out front playing checkers on the porch, reminiscing about the old days and shaking their heads at the way the world had changed.

A plain-white box truck was idling on the edge of the parking area, its motor sounding in need of coffee. Lance walked around the truck and then leaned against the side of the building, pulling his cell phone from his pocket and making an important call.

"Still alive?" Marcus Johnston asked when he answered the phone on the second ring.

"Still alive," Lance said and then told him everything he could about Diana and the girls selling sodas and their terrible circumstance.

Marcus listened silently the entire time, and when Lance had finished, the man simply said, "I'll make some calls, see what I can do. And I'll make sure this girl—Diana—I'll make sure she's safe. At least as long as she's here."

And that was all Lance had hoped for. Just to give Diana and the rest of the girls a chance.

"Coming home yet?" Marcus asked.

Lance shook his head. "Not yet."

"Stay safe, friend."

And the call was over and Lance went inside to buy some bottles of water and some protein bars. And then, because he told himself he'd do so before he officially left Sugar Beach for good, he ordered a softshell crab sandwich, which the lady behind the counter delivered to him wrapped in wax paper. He scarfed it down in four bites as she watched apathetically, and then he smiled and told her it was very good.

He used the restroom, and when he came back outside, there was a man standing by the driver's door of the box truck who asked, "Need a ride, son?"

He looked to be in his early fifties with a receding hairline and big, kind eyes. He was wearing golf shorts and a baggy t-shirt and looked completely at ease with anything and everything—as if "agenda" was a foreign word.

"I saw you walking," the man said. "When you were coming down the road, I mean." He shrugged. "Thought maybe you'd like a lift. I'm going another two hours north. You're welcome to join me. Always nice to have company."

Lance was about to answer, but his cell phone buzzed in his pocket and he stopped to pull it out. Looked at the screen and saw her name.

"Hello?"

"Where are you?" Leah asked. "Still in Sugar Beach?"

"No."

"Well, where are you going? Because ... because I've left Westhaven."

And there was silence, filled with lots of unspoken words between the two of them as the truth of their relationship took hold. Lance looked at the man by the box truck, who was waiting with eyebrows raised and a smile on his face. He heard the words the spirit of the girl with the red hair had spoken to him on the beach as they'd sat around the fire, about not having to do it all alone.

"I don't know yet," Lance said, giving a thumbs-up to the man by the box truck and starting to walk toward him. "But I'll let you know when I get there."

Thanks so much for reading **DARK SHORE**. I hope you enjoyed it. If you *did* enjoy it and have a few minutes to spare, I would greatly appreciate it if you could leave a review on Amazon saying so. Reviews help authors more than you can imagine, and help readers like you find more great books to read. Win-win!

-Michael Robertson Jr

For all the latest info, including release dates, giveaways, and special events, you can visit the page below to sign up for the Michael Robertson, Jr. newsletter. (He promises to never spam you!)

http://mrobertsonjr.com/newsletter-sign-up

Follow On:

Facebook.com/mrobertsonjr

Twitter.com/mrobertsonjr

More from Michael Robertson Jr

LANCE BRODY SERIES

Dark Vacancy (Book 4)

Dark Shore (Book 3)

Dark Deception (Book 2.5 - Short Story)

Dark Son (Book 2)

Dark Game (Book 1)

Dark Beginnings (Book 0 - Prequel Novella)

OTHER NOVELS

Cedar Ridge

Transit

Rough Draft (A Kindle #1 Horror Bestseller!)

Regret*

Collections

Tormented Thoughts: Tales of Horror

The Teachers' Lounge*

*Writing as Dan Dawkins

Printed in Great Britain
by Amazon